Hardly Working

HARDLY WORKING

A Semi-Auto Fiction

By Caleb Caudell

Published by Bonfire Books,
753-755 Nicholson Street
Carlton North, VIC 3054, Australia
info@bonfirebooks.org
www.bonfirebooks.org

ISBN: 978-0-6457768-7-4

A catalogue record for this book is available
from the National Library of Australia

Cover photography: Kiwi Cap & Bathurst Edwards

Also by Caleb Caudell:

The Neighbor
Novelty and other stories

Hardly Working

YOU DON'T KNOW WHAT YOU HAVE UNTIL YOU SEE SOMEONE ELSE WITH MORE

THE LANDLORD COULDN'T FIX THE FURNACE. I slept in my coat and slippers under two blankets with a fat cat by my side. Reminded me of camping late in the year. Snug in a sleeping bag on hard dirt and stone. I never slept well. I'd be up before anyone else, thinking about the cruelty of nature, stirring ashes with a stick as the morning light splintered the sky.

When I wake up, I know the day will be good for nothing, I'll survive on the strength of impersonal will. Moving, speaking, smiling; all unconscious and dulled. When I'm tired I'm numb to everything but my exhaustion.

Two repair guys came to the house and they couldn't fix the furnace. I spent the night at my boss's place. His wife is a lawyer. They have more spare bedrooms than the total number of rooms in my house. I slept for six hours and went to work. At five in the morning I made iced coffee. Later, I burned my thumb on a baking tray.

The café where I work serves cocktail inspired coffee. I make lattes with six steps and three garnishes. I've been wearing the same pair of shoes for the last five years. When it rains my socks get wet and my feet smell like a feedlot.

The man who lights an orange peel over your drink lives in a heatless house and shits in a doorless bathroom. The product hides the grime of the worker. And I'm doing better than most, by global standards. My own lowly station rests on the backs of even lower laborers; the flannel shirt I'm wearing was stitched by an enslaved Chinese child.

I abandoned my house and the landlord didn't try to stop me. She asked me not to tell her ex-husband because he'd let his ex-girlfriend live there. Now I'm living out of a bag. This weekend I'm going to my parent's house as temperatures drop below zero again.

Skin splitting winds, air that will chap your sack. I need to find a place with doors and a working furnace.

Compared to where I'd been living, the place looked like a palace. The bathroom had a door and the furnace worked. There was a big backyard and a two-car garage. When I went for a tour I didn't see anything suspicious. The landlord talked about a new carpet, a new bathroom and new lights. He didn't say anything about one neighbor selling crack and the other selling heroin.

Moving in that first day, I saw three people on the lawn to the left. They had skin like old parchment paper and wore shirts with oil stains. They welcomed me and my girlfriend to the neighborhood and asked if we needed any help. We told them we were fine.

People came by all day looking beaten and haggard, as if they'd been rolled down a rocky hill. Sometimes they knocked on my front and back doors and asked for a guy named Elvis. I'd send them one house over. Rusted trucks and old vans idled on the sidewalk and rumbled off. I'd hear arguments; assbeatings routinely promised. On the porch of the crack house they'd sit and stare into nothing, gibber and smoke cigarettes.

The guy who sold heroin owned a landscaping business and I paid him to cut my grass. I thought he would interpret me buying a lawnmower and cutting my own grass as a betrayal. He overcharged but I didn't feel like bargaining. I figured it was better to be gouged financially than gouged some other way. He did a good job with the lawn.

I liked the inside of my house but the neighborhood

brought me down. Pig-faced women bellowing at their bastard kids. Shirtless forty-five-year-old men on tiny bicycles, pedaling with unlaced Timberland boots. Every lawn was a junkyard, with broken mowers and grills and primer-colored cars on flattened tires sinking into mud. Toothless, grey-haired hookers shambled up and down the street two blocks west.

The neighborhood was developing. Among ranch houses with trash bag-covered windows and dirty plastic toys on the porch, there would be a brand-new house designed by an alien. Just beyond the rundown streets a new distillery or brewery opened every month. New coffee shops, gastropubs, bars where twenty-eight year-old men with the hairstyles of Viking warriors ate postmodern French fries and picked drinks from a list of 4,000 microbrews.

I lived for two years in that house between the two drug dealers. Listened to all the fights. Heard the crying and screaming and rattling laughter. Answered the door and talked to people too strung out to stand up. People swaying on lawns and porches in the mornings when I left would still be there when I came back. A few months before my lease was up that second year, after I'd decided to leave, the heroin dealer moved out and the crack dealer was beaten to death in his living room with a baseball bat.

A crackhead stole my backpack just before I moved out. For two years I lived between two drug dealers, including the one beaten to death with a baseball bat but nothing bad happened to me until my bags were packed.

Someone stole my backpack that happened to hold my laptop that happened to store two stories I'd been writing over the last six months. One was 50,000 words and the other 30,000.

We're supposed to sympathize with the underclasses but I dream about bulldozing them into a ditch. I had to get out of Indianapolis. Urban life is for young singles with money. The city shines with the promise of pleasure, night after night of novelty. At first it electrifies, then it comforts, and then like all things it falls into tedium. The traffic and noise, the faces and bodies, the routes from home to work to stores and shops.

Life in the city is a shelling of the senses. Crashes, booms, honks, shouts. Concrete and steel, trash, shootings and stabbings, the smell of sewage, hobos reminding you you're one mishap from passing out on a park bench covered in pigeon shit. In the city you need sandwiches with ten kinds of spicy mayo to feel alive. You need an electronic force field protecting you from all those sights, smells and sounds. You must walk fast, drive fast, talk fast and declare your love for diversity while screening out hordes of strangers.

So tired, but what does it matter? Tired or not tired, either way I'm tired. I sleep when I should stay awake and clench when I should sleep. The present barricades the past. The longer I live the less I remember. The more I've lived the less I am. It's not only the distant past that haunts me; I miss the self I was last week. This morning is as dead as my childhood. Defining moments lose their definition. Carried by a conveyor belt, fed into a furnace. The consolation of clichés. The modern method of transcending death is forgetting about it.

I moved to North-Central Indiana right before the corona virus. I'll never go back. I'll move farther into the country. Now I'm in a small town. Soon I'll move into the woods and squat among the toads.

The unpopulated expanse gives my soul room to roam. I love the flatlands, the faraway horizon. The quiet mornings. I can walk around without a million people crawling up my ass. Drive for miles without getting caught in traffic. See cows, horses, llamas and emus grazing on the plains. Watch hawks wheeling in the blue sky.

In my twenties I worked in fashionable restaurants and cafes. Now all those places are closed. The people who worked there are out of a job and the people who frequented them are out of a latte. They act as if Armageddon has arrived because they can't go out for flaming cocktails.

I work in a Wal-mart distribution center now. They pay their warehouse workers a decent wage. Not by the standard of what wages should be when adjusted for inflation. Not by the standard of what we could negotiate if we had strong unions and labor movements. Those days are gone and they're never coming back. The population is too big and fractured for working-class politics.

Now would be the time for Wal-mart workers to unionize and demand higher wages and better benefits. Workers in the warehouse should make thirty dollars an hour. The borders are closed and a third of the population was bedridden before the virus. Another third breaks a sweat when pressing buttons on a vending machine. The final third thinks they should be paid to talk about David Lynch movies.

Who in America right now will undercut the wages of men and women willing to work ten-hour days stacking boxes in the heat and cold? We could find out if the Waltons have a bit more to spare, if consumers will spend a little more for the privilege of shuffling through a supermarket in their Tweety Bird sweatpants to buy pancakes on a stick. But I'm sure Wal-Mart has legally protected itself against unions, negotiation of wages, strikes and protests.

In reality, this is as good as it gets. I can make twenty dollars an hour working in a warehouse or I can sit on my ballbag hoping someone will pay me to write about tv shows that encourage black girls to become space detectives. Or I could work as an assistant adjunct guest lecturer at Budweiser Tech online university or sell watermelons from a wooden stand. I didn't make the world I was born into and I can't design it according to my tastes and aspirations. I can either work with what's available or take another bong rip and wonder why I'm not getting paid to analyze the fascist subtext of *Thomas the Tank Engine.*

Capitalism isn't the primary reason we're fat, unloved, alone, tired, broke, untalented, riddled with autoimmune disorders and sexually transmitted diseases, bald, hairy, ugly and working jobs that stifle our unique human potential. No matter the system, we won't earn a living with our painfully personal poetry, our novel about a nitwit who struggles to write a novel about a nitwit, our indie electronic dreampop dance music, our period blood paintings, our necrophagists who brunch podcast, our Satanist cookbooks and feminist urinal cakes. A lucky few are born into money and can afford to piss their time away writing or tweeting or sculpting religious figures sucking their own dicks.

In a perfect world we could spend all day plaster-casting our pussies and eating ho hos while crowds called us a genius, and no one would ever feel ugly and depressed. But Satan rules the fallen world and we're sinful and disgusting beasts. I'm reminded of a passage Marx wrote, where he describes the upcoming communist society: an emancipated person would hunt in the morning, fish in the afternoon, rear cattle in the evening and criticize after dinner.

I can't imagine the average communist of today hunting and fishing and rearing cattle. By the look of things, the contemporary communist itinerary is dinner and criticism all day long.

GETTING BY

IT'S SEVEN IN THE MORNING and I've been awake since two AM. I'm sitting in the break room at the Walmart distribution center, a massive rectangular building surrounded by semitrucks. First shift is four AM to two-thirty PM, Tuesday through Friday. Workers get a twenty-minute break at seven, a half hour lunch at nine-thirty and then a fifteen-minute break at twelve-thirty. I drive a hydrogen powered forklift that weighs more than a car. I stack boxes of food and drinks up to seven feet high and take those stacks to a shrink-wrap machine.

The interior of the compound is composed of long aisles lit by fluorescent tubes on sky-high ceilings. One part of the building stores dry goods, shelf stable items: snacks, cookies, breads, crackers. Another part holds the fruits, vegetables, dairy and deli goods, where the temperature is set at thirty degrees. The last section is the freezer, with a temperature of negative ten and a subsection for ice cream at negative twenty. I work in the freezer.

Machines drone at a deafening volume. I wear a headset and a robot woman orders me to pick a certain number of boxes from a pallet slot on a shelf. I stack the boxes on the pallet carried by the forklift and move to the next slot. When I pick the last box on a slot, I carry the seventy-pound pallet to a loading station. My clothes freeze, the hair on my face freezes. Ice encrusts my brows and lashes. My body stings all over. It's a cold that kindles demonic hatred. I want to lay waste to heaven.

If I don't stack the boxes in a tight pattern my stack falls apart. Then I have to pick up the boxes and restack them, sometimes using tape to hold them all in place. My feet and fingers scream with pain. For three months I'm expected to increase my rate of order filling until I can consistently hit one hundred percent. I don't know what it means to pick at one hundred percent. It's probably some calculated percentage of boxes in a day that guarantees a certain profit. If I don't stack the correct number of boxes with maximum efficiency, then a woman in Wichita will only get two tubs of Lucky Charms ice cream.

Ours is the fattest plague population in history, with an

economy that buries us in boxed food. If you run out of toilet paper you can wipe your ass with a hot pocket. If you lose your house you can build a new one out of Marie Callender pies.

At seven in the morning, after three hours of stacking boxes, I'm so tired I need someone else to sleep for me. Then I discovered Starbucks brand triple shot caramel energy drink. It comes in a girthy aluminum can. It has caffeine, sugar, guarana, ginseng, guano, bull semen and other oriental ingredients believed to supercharge virility. It tastes like deck sealant but it gives me energy to finish my shift.

I don't know if I still have a job at Walmart. For the last two days I haven't gone in or called them. They haven't called me. I just got a letter from HR congratulating me on getting hired.

The hours, the environment, the clothing: all of it haunting. I worked there for a month and the thought of that robot woman's voice sends a chill over me. *Slot 245. Pick 2. Slot 247. Pick 1. Slot 254. Pick 12.* The bottom half of my ski mask frozen solid. My toes and fingertips tingling. The stabbing horns like pianos in hell. Roaring refrigerators, whirring shrink wrappers, banging machinery, vacant men at the wheels of forklifts, pirouetting in a grotesque industrial ballet. The tedious stacking of boxes, the seven-foot-tall mounds teetering with every turn.

If it were just stacking boxes in a uniform manner then I could let my mind go. But I must concentrate on the monkey puzzle of stacking boxes of wildly different sizes and weights. Sometimes two pallets, seven feet tall; boxes that weigh fifty pounds, twenty pounds, one pound, huge rectangles, long thin tubes. The pitiless robot woman tells me what to do. She hears I've picked the correct number of boxes. She's deaf to my misgivings. Sometimes I start a trip in the middle of an aisle, picking up tiny pies until I have a five or six-foot-tall stack, and then I hit the sixty- pound chicken breasts.

I hated that job from the start, but I might be soft. They imply as much. *Well, we have people who can do it, so obviously it can be done.*

I take it all back, what I said about physical work and contributing to the economy. If my fate was drudgery, then why the coddled upbringing, the investment of resources in intellectual and cultural development, the expensive and elongated education?

I grew up in carpeted institutions. Always learning from a book, always reading about another life, someone else's work, and then writing about what I'd read. Learning, memorizing, reading, speaking, getting graded, pleasing parents, pleasing teachers, studying strictly defined subjects for exact spans of time. Someone got me up and put me on the bus; someone put me in a chair, told me to read, to write, to memorize this, understand that; prepared me for tests, for more sheets of paper on my desk, pencils and erasers, sitting and scratching into column after column of bubbles.

They said my mind was my identity and the key to a comfortable life. It's an information economy; a test-taking economy, a class-based economy. I was born into a class with the privilege of always being in class, reading books, writing about books, reading and writing about books written about reading other books.

I sat at desks listening to lectures, thinking, reviewing, analyzing, memorizing as pencil shavings piled up, and then I relieved myself in bathrooms cleaned by lummoxes. I walked in parks pruned by a race of dwarves.

Why did I sit at desks for nearly twenty years, reading about the Greeks, the Romans, the Magna Carta, photosynthesis and cellular mitosis, Gregor Mendel and Pasteur; why did I read Shakespeare and Dickens and Hemingway? Why did I learn to read? I suppose my free time is when I should enjoy the fruits of an education in the humanities. I should cultivate my soul and read Virginia Woolf and Heidegger in those hours after work when I'm so tired I can't follow the plot of America's Funniest Home Videos.

The forty-two-year-old man who trained me at Walmart has worked in the warehouse for seven years. He said: *you're overthinking it. You just do the same thing, day after day. Act like a zombie.*

Like a zombie. To make it in this world I need to eat my own brains.

CHARITY AT SCALE

I HAVE A NEW JOB NOW, a new job again. Looking to make a few weeks of training money and then quit. Eligibility specialist for a private company contracted by the state, supplied with staff through a temp agency. Our tax dollars pay intermediaries to share information.

Determining eligibility for food stamps. Medicaid and other government programs. Helping our nation's most vulnerable. Those most disproportionately affected by poverty, crime, homelessness, underfunded educations, food deserts, eating too many desserts, drug abuse, sexual abuse. Orphans, runaways, boxcar children, underage prostitutes. All the orphaned underaged obese prostitute runaways beaten by their deadbeat stepdads living in boxcars in a food desert in the Mojave Desert. I'll be processing claims for TANF and SNAP.

The job is talking to people on the phone, getting their information and putting it into a computer. It should take thirty seconds to learn. We're taking a month because there are multiple operating systems and procedures and applications. A long list of programs. IEDS and IECS and EED and FFR. Navigation bars, menus, screens, policies, handbooks and rules. I'm not supposed to provide information on cases to anyone. Or judge the applicants. I'm not to let my personal feelings about applicants skew my handling of their cases.

Eligibility specialists work on government websites from 1994. We use DOS. The programs are always updated but the basic system is from the beta internet days. No, we don't use ICES anymore, now it's IEDS. DOOF is now DINK and will soon be subsumed by DORF. Functionaries earn a salary to shift letters of departments and systems around, to create anagrams with agencies; IEDS is now DIES, but I'll still work on a big grey box computer built in 1988.

Eight hours a day training in a class of over one hundred people. Four weeks of working from home and then we go into the office. People like the idea of working from home, but they ignore its downsides.

Commuting is torture, scientifically proven, and an office turns a man into a castrated hamster. But the modern home is a fallout shelter in a radioactive social world.

Sitting at home alone, or seeing your wife and kids, or your wife's kids, your wife's boyfriend and his boyfriend or girlfriend, doesn't make up for the absence of public life. Most people don't have enough socially structured hobbies or obligations outside of work. Eight hours of Call of Duty in fart-perfumed pajamas can't replace the missing connections of a physical workspace.

Although it may appeal to a man's selfish instincts to sit in sweatpants and type on a computer in a locked room while gnawing on a turkey leg, he's spiritually, civically and morally improved by embodied interactions, by spending time in public space.

The relaxed fashion and behavior in the home may seem preferable to the formalities of the office, but the current resentment toward a public standard of appearance indicates widespread maladaptation and stunted maturity, a pathological obliviousness to others and a decline of outwardly directed behavior in professional and collective settings. We dress like refugees and mental patients because of mass-produced sleepwear and because we're not expected to cultivate self-respect or restraint. We don't value bodily comfort—obesity and chronic illness ravage the body, bad choices trouble the soul.

People wear comfortable clothes in public because they're uncomfortable, because their bodies are panicked and inflamed from decades of nutritional and emotional chaos. Modern hedonism violently contradicts the sagely approach to moderating passions and limiting pleasures. Unrestrained eating, drinking, drug intake and consumption of media implies hatred of the body, not love of the senses.

Apart from cutting out the commute, working from home reproduces the corrosive tendencies of modern life, driving them farther along the path of social and spiritual disintegration. Sitting alone in a living room talking to scattered shut-ins on a computer while wearing synthetic fabrics made in Southeast Asia isn't an escape from the deadening routines and depressing trends of the present, it's their fulfillment.

RAINY DAYS AND MONDAYS

IN THE PRESENT, sexuality has been replaced by masturbation. Eroticism alleviates the stress of an overworked and overstimulated psyche.

Free sexual expression is a core value of vitalistic philosophies that claim to exalt life as discharge of energy. But the unmooring of sex from reproduction leads to extinction. By focusing on the freedom of an organism to release its energy, the philosophy of sexual liberation condemns society to death.

People live as isolated currents, and they renounce their legacies.

Grey skies and pattering rain. Late afternoon but it feels like morning. Leaves fall to the ground but time doesn't pass. Yesterday I went hiking in a state park with a friend. A friend who happens to be a woman. The colors of the leaves are changing, almost ahead of schedule; the atmosphere is expectant. A moment of passage, an ephemeral in between. Neither summer nor autumn. Warm and windy, a hint of decay.

We walked on dusty shaded paths over roots and stones, under tall trees and red and yellow leaves. Around other people. Can't avoid them. They wanted to experience beauty just as we did. They have the same right to be there. Except for the ones who play music from their phones. They should be sent to a gas chamber.

We stood on the rocky shore of a lake and listened to the gentle waves. Sunlight shimmered on the water and gulls flew overhead. Eternity veiled itself in a moment, in the interplay of impressions. All appearances remind me of what never appears.

Then, later, lying in bed, a breeze blowing into the room through the open window like a sigh. The feeling of her fingers, her nails grazing my forearm. Eyes like I've seen before, like

I've never seen before. Deep and dark and aflame. Reincarnation is real: I've died and come back many times. I remember this happening; it's another first time.

Then I wonder how and why we lose this feeling, why it's no longer enough to look at someone and hold them at the waist, to lie in bed in the breeze with the light leaving the sky. Above the busy street and the stream of strangers. Why we have to look for someone else, why we empty out so quickly. We pass through people like shadows. I've loved before but this isn't the same love.

I was supposed to get married and have kids, move to a small town, mow the grass and toss hotdogs on the grill. Here I am in studio apartments, in the city, with women I know without knowing.

How do I correct this ungainliness of existence, this off-rhythm dance? The right person at the wrong time, the wrong person at the right time.

I meet so many people but I hardly meet anyone. Most of them might as well be wallpaper. But then I do meet someone. The way they look at me and touch me, it's as if I've always known them. I wasn't meant to do this, to play with passion year after year under shifting skies.

I woke up without knowing if I'd slept. Coming into a dream or out of one. She sat on the side of the bed and drank water from a glass on the nightstand. Streetlamps colored the room with grey light.

My throat felt like someone had hit it with a hammer. My

body like someone had run me over with an asphalt paver. Drank too much.

Something happened to me last night and is still happening this morning and this afternoon and this evening. Last night lingers on my face, its shadows stick to my eyes. It's almost the next night and I'm seeing her again.

Every time she says she wants to see me I can't believe it. Each time she asks *what are you doing tonight* I ask myself if this is real. Is this happening again? When will I go back to my soul clawing at the glass of its panoramic isolation.

That morning she got ready for work and we kissed in the ashen light. I left her apartment and drove around and went to this new breakfast joint opened by a guy I used to work for who fired me.

Under silver clouds I ate some hashbrowns and a sausage egg and cheese sandwich. Warm fall winds blew napkins from my table. Then I went to the coffee shop where she works and drank espresso and edited my novel and we talked when she had a break. I'm telling myself do not lose your head.

From the first kiss in the dusk on the steps of her apartment to the next week hiking up the highest hill in the county and looking down on the treetops, with the waving leaves and bracing wind and drab swirling sky, and then later in her apartment and my dick inside her like it belonged there—I've been telling myself don't lose your head.

But I want to lose my head. I want this thing to pop off like the cork of a champagne bottle. I want to forget everything but her lips and eyes and her nails digging into my shoulders.

I met up with her at her friend's house and I thought maybe we'll be cool, maybe we're all just friends here. Within an hour we were sneaking off to make out. Even then I thought: she's spending the night with her friend and I'll kiss her a little and then I'll leave. We can run away to make out like twenty year-olds at a basement show, but still, the night will end and she'll go to sleep and I'll go home.

Everyone else went home or fell asleep. We fucked on the couch like a comet was about to hit the house, like nothing else would ever happen.

I made it through the blurry buzzing week and on Friday I'm with her again. We got pizza and a bottle of wine and walked through her neighborhood, down streets with an esplanade and fountains and sculptures of lions and deer.

The streetlamps glowing and crunching leaves under our feet and the chilled evening air. Drinking from the bottle and holding each other walking and talking.

We saw an old man and woman sitting silently on their porch and she said she doesn't want to be like those couples that never talk and I thought, *I'll talk until I pass out to keep you,* but then I also thought *someday we'll have nothing to say.*

Two weeks later she stopped texting me. When I finally heard from her she sounded like someone else. Texting with this clinical language. Like an official document written in the official style. *Due to a processing error, we cannot query your request.*

Two weeks passed. I told myself I needed clarity even though I knew. A few more days went by and she got back to me, said we can meet up and talk. The next morning we got coffee and talked about her paid time off and where she might go and what she might do and I gave her advice. Told her to go to Grand Rapids, Michigan. A beautiful city with historic neighborhoods.

She was taking pictures of her drink and messing around on instagram and I was wondering what the hell happened. What was all that walking through the woods and the greying light and the wind in the leaves and us lying on the ground getting lost looking at the graphite sky; what was that, did I dream it, am I dead, am I in hell and have I been given love to feel it slipping out of my hand time and again?

Is that how it goes these days? Or any day from the beginning to the end, because no matter how solid something feels it's all smoke and shadow, and the best you're going to get is a feeling of forever that lasts a second or two, because every lover leaves, and when they stay then it's the love itself that leaves you both and you're looking at each other with a shared question that splits you apart: what was all that, did we dream it?

SCRATCHING SHAPES INTO THE ASHES

I HAVE TO WRITE ABOUT LAST WEEKEND before the week shoves it out of my brain. Before time takes my treasured experience to the landfill. Already too late. Memories like casings; skin of a sausage, used condom on the curb. What lives in me I can't keep. What I keep is a bone ripped from a rotting body, a fossil with lines that lose their legibility by the day.

I sway in the gap between experience and its artifact. Arrange the impressions, lay out the string of scenes. The trouble is—most of what I live isn't pictured.

❧

We play with the words and impressions and scratch shapes into the ashes after the fire dies down. Are we doing what we want or what we think we want?

We've never spoken on the phone. We've talked for hours in her bed. In grey light filtered by white blinds above traffic tearing through black night. Hanging over smokey snow under lonely lights in cold space. Talked until our last words leave our lips like the body and soul's submission to death.

She called after work. Her cat is going to die. I consoled her. A few hours later she called and said they put the cat down. I was going up there Saturday night to stay until Sunday evening.

I drove up Friday. We ate lasagna and drank wine and lay in bed and she talked about her cat dying in her arms. Eyes open when she died, the strangeness and the tenderness of it, the mix of guilt and relief. And me, and us, and not knowing what to do or say or feel about any of it.

Saturday morning we made coffee and then she went to work. I stopped at a couple cafes and didn't get much done. Every place annoyed me. The music was loud and people were shouting. A woman next to me stared at her phone and lifted her latte in a robotic pattern. Out of the side of my eye I watched the arm and the cup moving like a mechanical billboard. I wanted to headbutt my laptop.

Late Saturday afternoon, sitting at her table near the door. She folded her clothes and we said nothing. Comfortable in the silence like a real couple.

The plated light through the windows, the silver spots on

the hardwood floors and shimmering waves on the walls. The blue sky beyond and the cars on the street below like a river. I tried not to look at anything, because seeing one thing is blindness to everything. My eyes found her figure and there was nothing else.

Saturday evening, we went to a tiki bar owned by a man who also owns a coffee shop where I used to work until he fired me because I stopped filling out the opening and closing checklists, and one day I forgot to put a bus tub under the drain tubes of the espresso machine and backwater leaked onto the carpet of the renovated building, a German-American historical landmark and a former gymnasium for nazi calisthenics.

We drank wine and smoked weed. Drove through the icy night and went to the bar, got a table in the center of a dark room.

The burger was salty and the cocktails overpriced. We sat in oil-painted shadows and dabs of soft light sliding on the table, in some other world hanging and swaying and pulsing, cut from the everyday. People around us like cave paintings, nothing to me but faded pigments.

We went to her apartment and lay in bed and talked and fell asleep. Then Valentine's Day. I heard snow was coming that evening. We talked and agreed I should go home that afternoon. I packed up my things and got ready to leave. A moment later I was in bed with her.

We agreed to spend a few hours apart and then meet up again later.

Back out into the cold biting wind, under a sky stained pink and orange, the bare tree limbs stuck in dramatic poses like actors who've just been shot in old time westerns. Out among the cars and crowds.

Ninety-nine point nine percent of the world works the same, looks the same, sounds the same, all the time. The highways and city streets fill up with cars and then empty out and businesses open and close regardless of what happens, regardless of love and hate, wins and losses. People carry on with their tasks for the day and they carry on with their ageing and dying. Nothing will stop the rocking back and forth of the days and the rising and falling sun and the wind and the dust wafting through crowds of unseeing half-dreaming working miscellaneous someones.

HOLDING FAST TO THE FIRE

THIS EVENING, THE FALLEN SNOW shines brighter than the grey sky. Nothing moves except my soul, a shuddering without object, a feeling without beginning or end, an abstract median between two impossibilities.

My breath wakes the world; my thoughts shake the snow from frozen branches. By imperceptible shades, night creeps up from an abyss, and a black screen spreads over my bedroom window.

Always waiting, even when I arrive. The future tears into right now, eats the margins of the moment and gives life its significance at the cost of its wholeness. Turning off Interstate 65 onto Washington St, driving under the bridge and thinking then that I'll soon look back on this exact moment and cherish how happy I was to be almost where I wanted to be, right up against the edge of what I'd been looking forward to, in those sweet fleeting seconds before the realization of a dream that might be more joyful than the realization itself.

The weekend is over and I'm back in the week, back to work with a bent back, stooped like a buzzard, floating like a phantom through a holographic gallery. Stumbling through the cratered social landscape, shivering in the winter of civilization where the young fear for their lives and the elderly act like children.

In the coffee shop with distanced seating and limited indoor dining, safe eating and drinking. No promise of a better life, just more rules and regulations, the ever-increasing tempo of an improvised hokey pokey; the CDC says put your right foot out, turn around three times, wash your hands, put masking tape over your eyeballs, that's what it's all about.

Seven tables widely spaced and every one of them is one or two people on laptops. Theoretical human beings as I remember them but who knows behind six pairs of sweatpants and sweatshirts and fuzzy boots and puffy coats and oversized hats and multiple masks and goggles and black sunglasses.

Every person who walks into the shop looks like the Unabomber sketch. They could be hiding guns and knives and spray bottles of battery acid. No flow of commerce, no steady rhythm, just the silence of our shared distance shattered by an opening door. I stand ready to serve; I wait and then I get out a book and read two lines and then CAJUNKENKRAN KENEEERSHUNK the door opens and closes with a gothic theatricality.

Someone walks in with a backpack and a briefcase and a projector and an easel, a virtual reality headset, a kiln and a mound of clay, a stack of charts and graphs, water bottles and blankets and crayons and half the comforting objects and fabrics of their home, desperate to work outside the home while wearing a mask seated a safe distance from someone else so they can talk on zoom or skype to someone three hundred miles away alone in their home, bare-assed but wearing a blazer, a two piece suit above the waist and withered genitals tucked under the kitchen table.

I thought I hated people. But I've learned I don't hate them enough. In the old days, when I worked in shops and people came in and sat at the bar or hung around the counter and gathered at tables and flowed in and out in regular rhythms, when they stood and stared at me making their drinks, when they tried to chum it up with me, for all the annoyance I felt, for as exhausted as I thought I was, I had no idea it could get much worse.

Things are worse now because I have to stand and wear a mask for eight straight hours and wait for the occasional wraithlike entity to wander in and then I have to try and understand it from behind layers of cloth and a glass pane that makes every interaction feel like a prison visit. I ask for a person's name and when they talk it sounds like a wet fart hitting the back of their pants and with some of the masks you can even see the air blow the fabric forward with a little poof and the image nearly makes me retch.

"What's your name?"

"pffffshh"

"What's that?"

Then they spell it out, which is even worse.

"b r x e o e a o e u r u z"

"Just say the name, please."

In the old days I didn't hate people so much that I fantasized about humiliating them with masks and mandates and shouting at them to keep their distance and stay in their homes and cover their mouths. Looking back now, I miss the smiles of pretty women and the occasional interesting conversation from someone sitting at the bar or hanging over the counter.

At my shop the owner requires all patrons to keep their masks on unless they're actively eating and drinking. Even when seated at their table, if they're not in the middle of biting or sipping they must wear their masks over their nose. I'm supposed to watch people and scold them when they break the rules.

All my coworkers are women and they seem to have unlimited energy for reminding people of the policy and browbeating them when their masks fall under their nose or they sit and think and breathe with their filthy faceholes exposed between bites. *Sir could you please sir could you please, excuse me sir could you please just a reminder that our mask policy is that you keep it on unless.* Childless women act like daycare directors.

Now the CDC recommends two masks. My boss hasn't asked me to wear two while working, but she's stocked the café with disposable masks to be worn safely under a cloth mask that will have to be safely swapped for another cloth mask midway through the shift.

At this point I'd rather be dead. Life has to be more than shallow breath and rapid heartbeat and running like a rat through a fake wasteland between safe and deadly spaces. Go ahead and kill me if this is all we're going to do with ourselves.

Two nights later and I'm sitting by my window. Watching the silhouettes of trees against the sunset. In the time it takes to write this paragraph, the ruby light burns and then dies, leaving a purple afterglow. Gone forever out there but lingering in here; for a few moments clutched by my conscious mind and then stored for the rest of my ephemeral life, sinking down into my unconscious with every other flash of light and color and then dumped into nothing when I die.

But I'll never learn and I'll never change; I'll feel the same about the leaden shifts composing the greater length of my timeline; I'll grasp at the fleeing flames and wait for their return and remember the imagined triumphs when I felt I held them fast.

BLACK FRIDAY

TODAY IS BLACK FRIDAY. A day of Dionysian commerce. They call it Black Friday because sales are in the black, something like that. All stores lose money until the day when people punch each other in the head over discounted microwaves. Probably got its name from an atrocity. Some village of rugmakers was burned to the ground and the bones of babies were fashioned into musical instruments and garden tools.

The history of everything can be traced to rape,

enslavement and extermination. Behind everything warm and welcoming there's a pile of dead bodies, dispossessed peoples wandering the earth wearing sandpaper loincloths, driven from their ancestral huts by the flames of pale devils.

Before you savor those buttery mashed potatoes or look fondly into the eyes of your grandmother, please remember the floggings and broken peace treaties, the dreamers and mystics strung up and beaten with nail studded boards, the bloated bodies swinging in the wind, the charred corpses of medicine men buried under your suburban home.

DO NOT allow your idiot uncle to talk about turkey or football or the holiday season without reminding him of starving kids in barbed wire cages and the tattered teepees of dancing bison people, the maternal spirit of the earth weeping as shoppers court cardiac arrest running like loosed hogs down the aisles of a Best Buy.

Black Friday but the sales have been going on all week. Some stores open early, on Thanksgiving Day. Black Friday is on Tuesday or Wednesday, it's whenever we say it is. Order ahead, order online, order telepathically. No day is on the day it's on. Christmas is a month away but go ahead and deck the halls. Skip the line, skip the screaming children and adult children, the diabetic depressed socially distant consumers waiting for the latest gaming console. Calcified pineal glands, swollen colons, joints buckling under inflamed flesh, headed for shoulder replacement surgery and radiation therapy. Mood stabilized citizens staying safe and healthy and saving lives.

We now have less dignity than our computers. The solitary person is mutating into a sterile autist, obsessed with survival, maintaining solipsistic homeostasis through high-grade stimulation.

Today I will use the technostructure to order a piece of plastic to my home. I'm doing my part to stimulate the economy and buy crap that I will spike into a trashcan like a football in two months after it stops working, while keeping people safe by limiting my exposure to the outside world as much as possible—this makes me a hero. I have sores on my ass from sitting on the couch safely yelling at people. I have the pallor of a man with tuberculosis. I'm ready to sacrifice all embodied contact with other people, ready to eat myself into a coma in a windowless basement until science says the crisis is over.

THE PIERCING RATTLE OF EMPTY SHELLS

MORNING BEFORE WORK. I thought I had three days off but it turned out to be two. I needed those three days. I need five days, ten days, ten years, the rest of my life.

But I'll work almost every day. Everyone must work. The modern project of using science and reason to free humanity ends with everyone working and watching miniseries, writhing under godforsaken skies, pretending to find substance in a vacant universe.

You used to be a slave to a king. Then you were a slave to a boss. Now you're a slave to yourself, your contrived passions, your electrified impulses.

Today I work seven am to four pm. It looks like nine hours but I have the option of taking an unpaid hour break. Eight or nine hours. Still the greater part of the day, the greater part of my life. Most of the day pressing a button and taking orders and putting syrup and milk in a cup and asking each customer if they would like their drink short or tall, would they like their drink hot or iced.

How are you? In a Disneyworld version of hell. In a charming café with brick walls and subway tile and neon signs and tattooed girls in yoga pants and doughy men in athletic clothes and the same funk playlist every day. We're not allowed to play our own music. Curtis Mayfield and James Brown and four on the floor drumbeats. Horns wailing and a dead man on coke screaming about his boner while I put a chocolate croissant in the oven.

Every day I think I'll skip the break and make a little extra money or go home early but every day at eleven or twelve I take that break and I walk down to Subway and get a sandwich that tastes like rubber. I sit in the basement with all the paper cups and syrups and frozen pastries and I stare at my phone or I stare at the walls for an hour and I can still hear the grinder upstairs and it's like a Vietnam vet hearing helicopter blades.

I need to work less because I'd rather punch people in the face than serve them coffee but I need to work more because I'm barely making enough to afford the rent.

We broke up. Or she broke up with me. I want to say we so it sounds like a management decision. A bureaucratic procedure. We've come to an agreement on the termination of our partnership and are now taking the requisite steps to withdraw emotional and sexual resources.

Had the day off and I knew it was coming. Bad electricity in the air. Got my tax returns and tried to stay busy buying kitchen supplies. Bought light-blocking curtains for my bedroom and went to the gym.

We met at the fountain in the center of the neighborhood. Running water and chirping birds and evening breeze and her cold hard eyes, her cold quiet voice. Green leaves hanging over the streets and cars rolling by and families strolling along and the familiar anguish that still burns, a seasoned sadness.

No arguments, no dramatic scenes, no pledges to change. I agreed with her. But I should've ended it first so I could've felt more like a man.

At least I stayed cool when she said she couldn't do it. Didn't threaten to hurt her or myself or anyone else. Didn't punch an old lady or kick a dog or scream into a baby's face. I told her she could reach out if she needed anything but she'd never hear from me again. It made me feel better. A grain of self-respect in a sandstorm of degradation.

Then I had to work the Indianapolis 500 weekend. Even busier than usual. But I needed to feel numb. Ground down to a nub. Reduced to a function. Anything but feeling sad, anything but remembering, anything but the horror movie torture footage of happy moments gone forever. *Saturday evening on her friend's farm in the hills of southern Indiana. The cool air and crackling fire. Her childhood friends were getting married and we talked about getting married too. That night she drove me through her hometown, showed me her high school. Streetlights and gas stations under the tarpit sky. We come from the same place and we are the same person, except we don't know each other at all.*

Almost got into a fight with a guy who ordered a nitro cold brew and yelled that his drink was not a nitro because there was no foam. I wanted to throw him through the glass. Put my elbow into his teeth, drop a knee on his groin. Beat him to death with a chair. Run him through the dishwasher, put the steam wand up his nose and blast his brain with scalding water.

He left a bad review and that means the team needs to have a talk about hospitality. It isn't the forty thousand happy customers that matter, it's the one dickhead who didn't have a great time. The one mistake, the one flaw, the human weakness that gets all the attention, that defines you.

I hope I get fired and attacked by a swarm of African killer bees and sprayed by a skunk and assaulted by a hobo. Hit by a cement mixer. Trampled by a herd of wildebeests. I hope a piano falls on my head. May I slip into a sewer. May I be forced to fight the latest MMA superstar in a barbed-wire cage on a bed of spark plugs and chain saws. Never love again never touch another woman never like anyone never get close to marrying and having kids.

We were supposed to spend the summer together. Long bike rides. Hiking and camping. Fucking under the starry night sky. Fucking everywhere. The idea was to see how it goes for the rest of the year and then when my lease is up next March maybe we get a place. Maybe move out of the city. We talked about the names of our kids. I'm too old to start over again.

❧

After work on Sunday I drove home to my parent's house for a Memorial Day get together. Pulled into the drive and Dad was at the grill. Got out of the car and heard the ominous drone of the cicadas. The sound of blind life. Seventeen-year cycles; sleeping and waking and fucking and dying. There's nothing more than this, not even for us; human feeling is nothing more than the piercing rattle of empty shells.

Had a good time talking to my brothers and sister, my Mom and Dad. They're better people than me. Drove back to Indy in the evening and then she called. Said she wanted to take a walk. I should've said no. We slept together but I didn't spend the night.

These are the games of overgrown children in a senile civilization. Should be running a business or raising my kids. Instead I'm getting thrashed by desires while the world falls apart.

The next day she called. Then the day after that. And the next. Part of me is flattered but part of me is asking where is the nearest monastery? Where's my resolve? Where is the strength to lift myself above the whirl of passion?

All this work on the body. The weightlifting and bike riding and walking. The conspicuously branded self-consciously strenuous life, the Teddy Roosevelt simulacrum, the aping of a warrior. And still I give in to temptation. Maybe it's because somewhere in my soul I know this is all make believe, that nothing is more real in this realm of shadows than tingling flesh. No one cares what we do, not even ourselves.

Let the fountains be enough. The morning sun on the grass.

Evening walks in the shade. Still hours in the afternoon and peace in my heart. I felt a fledgling happiness. But God strangles joy in the crib. He doesn't want us to be happy. Or maybe it's me?

❧

She called one night around the first of August. After midnight, after a month without talking. I'd seen her at the neighborhood dive bar and she ran out of the room. A few days later I saw her coming toward me on the sidewalk and she crossed the street.

After the last time we talked I called her a soulless cunt. It was in a text. We were on the phone and she hung up on me. Life is one wrong turn after the next. Makeshift matter tearing itself apart. Can't get down to the cretinous core of what drives me.

Memories like airhorns in my ear. But each day opens with serene indifference. Getting up in the morning, walking on the warped wood floors of my apartment, soft summer light bleeding in through the blinds. Chirping crickets and singing birds. My clanking questions in the middle of a sonorous vale. The morning is music and my soul is noise.

Go over it again: rehearse what she did to you, replay your failures, review the moment you went left and then picture going right. What would've happened? You'd be together right now. On her couch, her head in your lap. Sitting in a chair turned away from the table, she comes to you from the kitchen. She floats into the space between your legs. Your hands meet her hips and you bring her in close. She bends for a kiss and time dissolves.

I missed her call that night but the next day we met. For the next few weeks she'd call or text and I'd go to her apartment. Her body makes me want to burn my life down. She says we're over, there's only one reason to see each other. Cut out every element but the carnal. No lazy evenings, no pizza and a movie. No morning coffee at the table. *We don't need to catch up.* We can do this because we know each other. Tried love and failed. We can settle for pleasure, enjoy our body parts. It never works. Human life is miserable in this way: we fall short of our ideals but we exceed our low expectations.

Mid-September, a stretch of hot sticky days. What they used to call Indian summer. Heat and humidity recalling July but the days are different now. The air has aged.

Late summer of my life. The mornings are still warm, moving still easy. Bound out the door without thinking. Soon I'll be cursing the cold but gratitude for what I have now escapes me. Try to live the present from the perspective of the future, in the mode of melancholic remembrance.

Biking down the potholed streets, heading west through construction zones. They're ripping up the streets, redoing the overpasses. Half the city is blocked off, detoured. Orange cones everywhere. I look behind me and catch a sunrise with the faded pink gleam of strawberry lemonade.

Another week, another weekend of work. Gencon convention. Understaffed coffee shops and restaurants struggle to serve the influx. Every fast-food place and department store and café is short of workers. Hiring signs on every storefront. No one works but everyone spends. An extended banquet, an orgy of consumption

❧

The problem of not having enough time is always secondary to having too much. The moment we're not in danger of death, we're tortured by boredom. Man can't sit still, and even when he does, he makes a show of it, turns it into a program, a philosophy. He makes stillness more work than it needs to be, attracts followers, people in need of entertainment.

The closest thing to a sage is the hobo who sits in the coffee shop, staring into the beyond for hours, getting up to ask for another free cup of coffee and then blast the bathroom walls with diarrhea. He's absorbed by his compulsions, mired in his indolence, caring nothing for status, recognition, the fruitless pursuit of being known by other nonentities.

He's always asking for something, but what he asks for can be given: a dollar, a cup of coffee, a sandwich, a cigarette. We, smug in our self-sufficiency, can provide these things for ourselves. But we want what people don't have and can't give, like love and understanding.

LEFT TO MY OWN DEVICES

I WAS BORN WITH A BROKEN DICK. It took me a long time to figure it out.

Sexual development is painful and disturbing in the best of circumstances, when nature has given us healthy bodies for the grim task of securing a mate. In my case, nature botched the job. Even as a teenager I struggled to get hard, even when alone.

My friends would talk of the ever-present threat of stiffening at the slightest touch, at the merest mention of sex.

They spoke of morning wood. I was aloof, and I didn't think much about the contrast between the stories of my friend's rigid members and my own weak and sporadic engorgement. I first heard the slang term boner from a boy on my baseball team, who told me it meant blood rushing into your dick. If their blood rushed, mine seemed in no hurry. Still, I didn't consider it a crisis, as I'd never been with anyone, nor did I intuitively know how I was supposed to work.

Around eighteen, I got a girlfriend. I'd go to her parent's house and we'd sit on her couch and watch movies. Fall semester of my senior year, driving on sloping backcountry roads, the sweet scents, the leaves bursting with color. Lit candles on the coffee table, the murmur of voices on the tv. We took it slow. Kissing for hours, our hands under blankets, pausing to talk and laugh, retelling stupid stories from the hallways, the parking lots and cafeterias.

One night her parents had gone out, and we went to her room and lay on her bed. She reached into my pants and put her hands on my soft penis. We undressed and I tried to jerk myself into an erection. Nothing happened. She didn't mock or scold. Her reaction could've been much worse, but the shame roasted me to the bone. It was an excoriating judgment that came not from her, or even me, but seemingly from an observational post that included the whole universe; I was exposed before all and found inadequate, malformed. The problem that defined my life had been laid bare.

My girlfriend and I worked out a system. I'd jerk off until I was hard enough to quickly push into her, and then I could last for a minute or two before I'd lose the erection or cum. Far from being a sex god or a king, I adjusted to reality as a crippled sex peasant. At least I'd lost my virginity.

At the same time, acid thoughts ate into me: *my girlfriend might like me, she might even love me for other qualities, my looks, my humor, my intelligence, but she needs a hard dick, a consistently hard dick. She can never respect or desire me because I fail the fundamental test of manhood.*

These days most people call it erectile dysfunction. Sounds like a mechanical problem. You picture blown gaskets, shooting steam. Erectile dysfunction sounds objective, as if it concerns something you might own, something with some practical value that doesn't effect your sense of self.

Formerly it was called impotence, a term that accurately describes how it feels to watch your dick wilt in front of a naked women. Impotence means a lack of power, an inability to fulfill your primary directive as a man. The broadness of the term increases its precision, because you can't separate sexual inadequacy from anything else. If you can't stay hard, if you wake up in the morning with a soft dick, you're not experiencing erectile dysfunction, you're impotent. Not only when you try to have sex, but throughout the day, in every act, thought and feeling.

From what I understand of history, men didn't talk much about impotence. In the nineties, a new drug arrived on the market. Viagra was originally developed as heart medication. Doctors found that it improved erectile capacity as well.

Advertisements of Viagra brought erectile dysfunction into pop culture; serious commercials aired among crass jokes on late night talk shows. The commercials featured elderly couples walking on beaches and sitting on porches, their eyes glowing with rekindled romance. Two angles were drawn by the popular imagination: erectile dysfunction was a side effect of ageing and an acceptable subject for mockery. The derision was lighthearted for the most part, but the message was clear enough. If you suffered from erectile dysfunction, you should seek help from your doctor, but people would laugh at you, think less of you.

It was assumed that young men didn't have this issue. The plumbing always works perfectly in youth and then degrades because of mounting systemic problems, diseases and conditions of civilization like hypertension, diabetes and prostate cancer. In a wealthy consumer society, men grow old and fat and bald and their dicks stop working. Fitting punishment for a life of indulgence.

(A consumer society commands people to enjoy themselves, to go balls deep in pursuing pleasure, and then castigates them for ending up sick, bloated and ugly. Worship of youth gives way to scorn for the infirmities of old age and the ravages of gluttony and lust. A young person is celebrated for his self-absorption, his appetite and energy, while an old man is ridiculed for clinging to his waning vitality, the only thing the social order has imbued with value.)

Today, we blame pornography for erectile dysfunction in young men. But in my youth people thought if a young man couldn't get hard for sex, he had performance anxiety. The problem was mental, not physical. One of the surest ways to give someone a mental condition is to tell them they have one. Though my penis barely worked even when there couldn't possibly be an issue of performance, the idea that my problem was in my head, that I was mentally responsible for the functioning of a body part integral to the greater life process, surely contributed to the warping of my mind.

Sexual medicine is much more sophisticated than it used to be. In the technical sphere, in treatment modalities, drug options and surgical techniques, progress is undeniable. In the seventies, a crude device was invented to cure impotence. Two malleable rods inserted into the erectile chambers kept the penis in a permanently semi-rigid state. Technically it works, though the drawbacks are significant. The penis is always harder than it would be when a normal man buys ice cream, but never as hard as it should be for penetrative sex.

At nineteen or twenty, I told my parents about my problem. I talked with a sex therapist. He walked me through relaxation techniques. I'm not sure he believed my problems were physical, but then he couldn't have done anything about that anyway. One doctor tried to test my nocturnal erections. I strapped an elastic ring to my penis; the ring was attached to a machine that would measure tumescence as I slept, but oddly enough I was unable to sleep, and I learned nothing.

Doctors prescribed Viagra and other drugs like Cialis and Levitra. The efficacy was limited. My dick would get harder a little faster, stay harder just a bit longer, but the problem remained. I still needed vigorous manual stimulation, and I'd lose my erection in the time it would take to put on a condom or change positions.

There were also side effects. My face flushed; I had throbbing headaches. The drugs open all your arteries. The slightly harder dick was counterbalanced by a feeling of nerve-wracking pressure all over my body, a tingling and creeping heat like a nineteenth century fever. Some men experience temporary blindness and lower back pain.

In the absence of a traumatic injury or compulsive porn usage, impotence in young men is now thought to be genetic. Sexual medicine specialists call it congenital venous leak. It refers to a genetically determined impairment of penile veins. An erection consists of two key moments: receiving blood and then trapping it. Arteries bring blood in, the tissues fill and expand, and a network of veins trap the blood, creating the pressure and firmness necessary for a durable erection. When the veins fail to cinch, blood flows in and then back out.

Venous leak affects around one to two percent of men independently of all lifestyle factors and accidents. The male population of the United States is roughly one hundred and sixty-three million; the number of men with congenital venous leak sits somewhere around one and a half million. Over a million men, yet I can all but guarantee every one of them feels like an isolated freak, an accidental pile of useless flesh.

Mass society raises the threshold for what counts as substantial and common while producing more frequent deviations. A million men with the exact same problem, dispersed among millions of others. The imagination can't represent a million, it's a dizzying quantity, but it's a disposable and trivial number in comparison with the total. I was almost thirty before I talked to another man with the same issue. Around the same time I talked to a doctor who specialized in a much more advanced practice of penile implant surgery.

※

My first girlfriend loved me despite my handicap. I cared about her but I had another problem in addition to my dick. I was nineteen years old and my hormones worked like a normal man. My testosterone production was at least average for my age, probably higher. I wanted to fuck as many women as possible.

If you want to understand the power of the male sex drive, especially in youth, consider this: At nineteen I was consciously aware that my dick would most likely not work in most sexual encounters, but I still felt an overwhelming urge to fuck. I went after any woman who showed interest.

My instincts worked like that of a starving man who chokes on the food he eats, but who then spends inordinate time and energy thinking of food, going out of his way to try different dishes, subordinating all other interests and occupations to the quest for a fully digestible meal.

This desperate and starving man could devise alternative feeding methods. A liquid diet. He could lower his expectations and content himself with small plates, meager meals. But imagine him prowling the streets, sweating in the kitchen, chomping on fatty sandwiches and thick stews, retching and howling and swearing at his misfortune.

If I'd had any wisdom, I would've stayed with my girlfriend. Accepted her love and loved her in return. But I hated myself. Consumed by loathing and desire, I pursued casual sex to confirm my power or abjection. if I was successful then I felt a minor uplift. If I failed then I wallowed in my anguish. Either way I'd get what I wanted.

I failed over half the time. When I could get hard enough for penetration I wouldn't last long. I kept trying. Shame and hatred and desire blackened my soul. No other interest seemed as important as establishing my sexual value, convincing myself that women didn't just love me, they loved my dick.

The penis is often called a tool, viewed as an appendage and a means to different ends. In my darker moments I think it's the reverse. The man is the tool that serves the dick. A man's life is the instrument by which the dick satisfies itself. A man will sacrifice his sanity, his resources, his time, for a shot of ecstasy. Risk his life and reputation for a few seconds of idiotic pleasure.

Nights would descend into a familiar scenario. On a young woman's bed, her on her back, me on my knees, between her legs. My ass clenched, jerking myself with one hand until I was sweating and shaking. Sometimes this worked; much of the time it didn't. Often I blamed it on alcohol, nerves, stress.

The women were mostly kind, but I could see the disappointment. Or at least I imagined it. How could I not? Women now talk about their reticence, their fear of upsetting potentially violent men. They increasingly speak of their silence. Participating in acts and pacifying a man's ego like they're trying to calm an escaped chimpanzee. How many times did women want to call me a freak, a loser, or express their own frustrations, their lack of enjoyment, but held back because they thought I'd punch a hole in the wall? I'll never know.

There was Kathleen. Freshman year in the dorms. She had a slender body, a tight round ass and red hair. A Chicago accent, her eyes gleaming with devilish heat. One night she suggested we go to my dorm to smoke weed. We lay in bed, vaguely high. She ordered me to kiss her. After making out, we undressed and I wedged my semi-hard dick into her for a few seconds.

We tried a couple times on other nights. A little while after that I asked her to come over and she said sex with me was too difficult. She could've been more insulting but it still hurt. Sex with me was difficult. Her sexual options were virtually limitless, so it was only natural for her to prefer an easier good time. Her comment highlighted the twisted nature of my predicament. Sex is supposed to be automatic, the most effortless, unconscious thing in the world, even to the point of being dangerous, in need of control, contrived limits. But I was difficult, achingly conscious of my bad reflexes, my busted motor; my sex was a labor.

For me, sex heightened my awareness of the arbitrary frailty of my body, strengthened my sense of myself as an isolated and crippled animal, some kind of mutant, a semblance of a man lacking the essential ability that defines him.

If you're impotent, you can take pills. You can use a pump to force blood into the penis and then close the veins with a cockring. You could also inject your dick with liquid vasodilators. Injections are effective but come with a risk of scarring that goes up over time. None of these methods are cures; they're treatments. There's only one cure.

With pills, you need to time it right. Take viagra roughly half an hour before sex. Cialis has a longer half-life in the body.

Take a pill that increases blood flow all over your body. Your face looks like you just ate a ghost pepper. Ignore the sweating and ringing in your ears, the headaches and back pain. Lug a penis pump with you to the club and hope for the best. Bring your medical briefcase with you on a date, keep the liquid vasodilator in the fridge, fill your syringe ahead of time. Get the girl naked and excuse yourself, go to the kitchen and shoot up.

(Technically, you have another option. Renounce penetrative sex. Join a monastery, take a vow of celibacy, devote yourself to God and good works.

The sexual revolution lowered the esteem of celibacy and chastity. In a religiously defined order, sex is a passion meant to be controlled by the spirit, directed to the institution of marriage or sublimated in service to God. Denial of sexual impulse affirms a higher power.

The sexual revolution enthroned sex, raised sexual pleasure to the highest good, the most vital purpose. If you're not made in the image of God, created to worship and participate in the glory of creation, endowed with a spirit destined for another realm, then all you have is tingling flesh, the technologically mediated pursuit of organic ecstasy. Only this one accidental life to experience as much gratification as possible, with no justification for restraint or spiritual compensation for failure.

Techno-vitalism is the animating principle of the current social system. A body or mind ill-equipped for sexual activity is now a technical project. Various social techniques and analytical programs fix behavioral problems, while manufactured devices and surgical interventions correct physical abnormalities.)

The only cure for erectile dysfunction is a penile prosthesis, implanted through a surgical procedure. A three-piece device, a technical object made possible by globalized economic development and applied science in the bio-medical industries. Division of labor and expert technique. The wonders of human ingenuity in service of a base aim, a primitive sexual power fantasy.

The cure is this: two inflatable silicon tubes, a pump and a reservoir filled with saline. The tubes go into the erectile chambers, the pump stays in the scrotum and the reservoir sits in the abdominal cavity, close to the bladder. When you press the pump in your sack, saline from the reservoir travels into the tubes in the penis. As the tubes fill up with saline, the penis hardens, expanding in girth and extending slightly in length, mechanically simulating a natural erection. When you're done using the device, you press a button on the pump that sends the saline back into the reservoir. The penis softens.

Everything is internal and undetectable by sight or feel, except for the pump, which is much harder than your usual set of nuts.

The sequence of penile implant surgery: first they give you antibiotics. Then they knock you out with an anesthetic. You're flat on your back, unconscious, in a black pit deeper than dreams, surrounded by doctors and nurses and sterilized equipment in a room of garish light. Masks and tubes and machines, readouts of vital signs, perfectly choreographed movements among the surgical team members. They've done this before and they'll do it again soon.

The surgeon makes an incision, either on the scrotum or the infrapubic region above the penis. From there he cuts open the erectile chambers and measures their length. Next he creates enough space to insert the inflatable tubes. Then the surgeon places the reservoir in the abdomen and tucks the pump in the scrotum between the testicles. Last he connects all three pieces with a network of tubes and tests the device, inflating and deflating it on the operating table.

In my early twenties I lived in a college town. I took classes and dropped out halfway through the semester two or three times. Women and friends were abundant, and there were parties and shows almost every night. My outlook went no farther than the next meal, the next high, the next fuck. Meals and drugs came easily; sex not as much.

Katy fluttered about in the same circles, showed up at the same bars and house parties. Her face was like the painting of a romantic genius; you'd think she'd driven poets to suicide. It wasn't only her face. Her voice and laugh were dazzling.

She went home with me one night after a party. We made out on my bed. I played Otis Redding and Curtis Mayfield on my computer. She reached for my dick and it was soft. I didn't explain and she didn't seem bothered.

We tried one other night. This time I went to her place. She came to the door in white lingerie and a silk gown. She'd opened the windows. The lights were off, the room was lit by streetlamps and the moon. A breeze flowed in like the shawl of a goddess. An evening cut from a marble dream smashed into pieces, not only by my unworking dick, but by the sense that I'd fail, that I shouldn't try, shouldn't be there.

(A strange condition, in which the drive stems from the penis, even though the penis can't secure its own pleasure, the purpose it sets for itself. Unless the drive camps in a dark corner of the soul rather than the physical organ. The insistence on satisfaction isn't primarily physical.)

I left a little before dawn in a haze of disappointment. When I texted her later she said nothing. We'd see each other at friend's houses, at grocery stores and coffee shops. She was always nice but she never invited me out or came over again. Even momentary gratification was outside of my control, and rather than renouncing sex or staying with a woman who appreciated me for other reasons, I threw myself into an embittering cycle of seduction and withdrawal.

Throughout my twenties I grew more obsessed with the impossible dream of basic sexual functioning. Whatever I accomplished, I was tormented by the fact that I couldn't do what was expected of a cretin. One particular year in my late twenties disappeared in a blur of internet research, speculation about cures and depressive rumination over wasted time. I replayed the awkward and embarrassing episodes and imagined the different courses my life would have taken had I not been cursed with impotence.

Everything around me deteriorated. I stopped going to the gym. My apartment overflowed with trash. On days off I didn't leave the house, sometimes spending hours in bed, propped against the wall, browsing forums and reading medical abstracts.

My biology had betrayed me. I felt in the deepest part of myself that I was unworthy of life. In much of the animal kingdom, the primary purpose of the male is insemination of the female. For many species, the male becomes useless after completing his reproductive goal. More complex species sometimes find a use for males in the child rearing process. But the male still has to impregnate, he still needs healthy organs. Evolution had judged me unfit for reproduction, as if my genetic code had given up on itself.

I saw vomit flying out of me. Before sensation returned to my groin I felt my stomach flipping and fire in my throat. My vision was blurry but the puke appeared as chunky liquid the color of watered-down coke.

Waking up from anesthesia; not like waking up as part of an organic cycle; more like being switched back on; abruptly coming out of a defenselessness much more extreme than sleep, in which the vegetative state of the body is entirely under the power of strange professionals and standardized procedures, in which the fundamental nervous condition of the body, its susceptibility to pain, is suppressed and managed by technical means. My dick had been sliced open and packed with foreign material. No other experience could have prepared me for the awareness of an inorganic object stuck inside my body.

Following the strange dull feeling of hard plastic shoved inside me, a sharp pain welled up in my crotch. A cheese grater against my dick, a hundred tiny buzz saws cutting into my flesh. I remember crying out and then a nurse giving me morphine.

The first two or three months after the surgery I regretted my decision. I was uncomfortable all the time. The first week

I had to stay on my back except for hobbling to the bathroom, getting into the shower and spraying piss everywhere. Pissing felt like someone taking a blowtorch to my dick tip. Boredom, discomfort, pain; time to think over the gravity of what I'd done to myself.

There was the brutal feeling of the hard object in my body. Like someone had rammed a broomstick into my crotch. I didn't have a dick anymore. It was a nail spike, the result of an industrial accident. I was some Phineas Gage of the little head. Unsettling personality changes on the way.

Early on, fear of infection loomed. No complication of penile implant surgery is more devastating. Infections occur in about one percent of cases, sometimes less, depending on the surgeon. An infected device must be removed. Sometimes they can immediately put in a new one, but most of the time they have to close the space and wait two or three months for another surgery. In that time, corporal fibrosis sets in, which will likely shrink the penis. Traumatized penile tissue will retract and harden unless stretched and kept open by the device.

All day I checked for signs of infection. When I felt warm I stuck a thermometer in my mouth. Every few hours I looked at the incision site and made sure it wasn't leaking pus.

At the time I had a girlfriend. Impotence didn't stop me from attracting women or earning their devotion. Most women lost interest after finding out my dick didn't work, but a few stuck around. I believe they loved me.

In those years love wasn't enough. I needed to know how it felt to kiss a woman without worrying how things would go.

I'd never known that ease, that unselfconscious animal

abandon; what appeared to me as the charm of sex, the stripping down of the conscious mind to reflex, the automatic exchange of pleasure. Maybe my idea of real or natural sex was a myth, distorted by bitterness and self-pity; maybe healthy men struggled to enjoy themselves, too. For years I could only suppose I was missing out on a crucial part of life.

(A sexually liberated society does away with sublimation. The unmasking of sexual energy as the basis of human behavior reduces life to the pursuit of pleasure. If sex defines and drives us, why not optimize our erotic experience and remove all barriers to enjoyment?

If the lowest urge is now the highest aim and the prime source of value, then a problem arises. What if a man still can't experience as much pleasure as he wants after tearing down all the old obstacles? The new man, psychological man, aware of his impulses, uninhibited, released from religion and morality, now has no compensation or excuse for failure to appease his appetite. Free sexuality imposes a brutal hierarchy; attraction bears no safeguards against predation, no consolations for defeat, rejection. Though the state can somewhat distribute resources, it can't administer sexual power, not without moral codes derived from religion.

Love and monogamy exert a more equalizing influence on sex than the notion that everyone should enjoy everyone else without guilt or jealousy. In the case of monogamy, people agree to renounce variety for security and the quieter fulfillment of a deepening bond. The supposed equality of uninhibited sexual exploration pits all against all, with no mediating principles or authority for settling disputes and no other values beyond experiencing the highest quality and quantity of pleasurable sensations.)

❁

Three months of discomfort and anxiety, of waking up in the morning and hoping my device hadn't broken through my skin, hoping the pump hadn't smashed my nuts. Monitoring for signs of infection, emailing my surgeon about redness or swelling.

Six months passed before I felt somewhat normal. My body finally incorporated the foreign object. I could activate the device and enjoy sex like never before.

The biggest benefit was the clarity of mind. For the first time in over a decade, I could think without reminding myself of my inadequacy. I had my surgery in the winter, and by late summer, not only was I having sex without pills, without shame and rage, I was sitting down to write, I was thinking and dreaming. I'd like to believe I could've transcended my desire for reliable sexual functioning and devoted myself to art, to God and family, but in truth that probably wouldn't have happened. Technical intervention was necessary.

My girlfriend and I broke up a few months later. Sex was the least of our problems. Even love couldn't save us. We had our passions and personality defects. It didn't help that I'd recently acquired new abilities. Still a fallen man, an especially greedy and selfish one, my rapid increase in power didn't lead to humility and gratitude, but higher expectations, hunger for a wider range of experiences. I wanted to impress as many women as possible with my technologically upgraded body.

❁

My penis relies on a machine, a machine that wears down and breaks. In a sense, no different from any other body, organic or otherwise. All organs process materials, converting one form of matter into another in support of the organism that holds all the parts together and coordinates their workings. Over time the organs decompose and vital movement ceases, the organism disappears into darkness without end. Other bodies with their organs come along and assimilate the dead flesh.

To be human is to resist organic cycles, to revolt against sickness and death. To augment our anatomy. We transform environments to suit our interests. The unnatural nature of technical power over matter unleashes its own torments, gives birth to our characteristic modern scourges.

New comforts and abilities bring fresh fears, novel illnesses, reactions upon reactions, scientific and medical innovations to counter the destructive effects of previous breakthroughs. No one guides us, no spirit or intelligence has given us a blueprint. We stand on the edge of nothingness, ashamed of our past and afraid of the future, yet we hope that one day we might engineer our happiness, organize ourselves into perfect beings.

The health and power of the modern man depends on a network of machines and a complex of techniques. His independent attitude draws its strength from the assumed reliability of innumerable devices and interrelated industries. At almost every moment, in everything he does, man is assisted by the unskilled labor of roiling masses, and he's improved by the brilliant insights of rare visionaries. Even when a machine stops working, it's taken for granted that it will be fixed. Each man does his part and ignores his enslavement to tools, techniques and the labor of others.

A man sleeps on a soft bed, wakes up with an alarm clock, flips on lights, shuffles about heated and cooled spaces and drives a car. He wears glasses to correct his vision and receives inoculation against diseases, takes pills to combat illness and pain. He receives nourishment from factory farms and works with tools made by others. And he overcomes boredom and banishes the terrors of empty time with an infinite store of entertainment.

Yet he rarely feels the insecurity of having outsourced his powers and multiplied his desires and overextended his interests. No sense of muscular weakness follows from using a bulldozer to move mounds of earth, no feeling of shame arises from buying food, no awareness of frailty builds up from taking vaccines and medication. Most people don't view themselves as deficient for being unable to entertain themselves, just as they don't despise their arms for being unable to send them into the skies.

I'm like nearly everyone in that everything I do ties me to machines, labor and expertise. But I've also had a machine installed within me, inside my most sensitive and intimate part. As soon as my body and mind adjusted to my new techno-sexual condition, it was as if I'd never lived the first part of my life with a crippled dick.

When going about my day, I don't feel the device within me. Even when I touch the hard pump in my sack, it feels natural, the feeling has been naturalized. The human spirit has two remarkable powers: invention and assimilation. Turning the old into the new and then turning the new into the old. The most abrasive intrusion into the body and the most violent disruption of habit are quickly absorbed and domesticated.

Almost immediately we lose our connection to old ways, our former agonies. The clanking of machines drowns out years of suffering. New technical programs revise our memories and beliefs in their own image, and the present stands ready to be erased by the future.

When I use my device, I don't think about my deficiency, about how this product of industrial labor and applied science restores a damaged function that we mostly view as primordial, prehistorical, outside shifting value systems. In the same way that the typical man doesn't lament his weak eyesight when he puts on his glasses or condemn the limits of his mind when making use of communication technology he doesn't understand, so I manipulate the tool within my tool without reminding myself of my original defect.

Man's prosthetics extend his possibilities and supplement his lacks while at the same time blinding him to his technical nature. Every increase in power is paid for by greater dependence on the continued operations of the technical system.

When my device breaks, the old inadequacy returns. The external event that happens within me forces thought to the surface. I have to think about my condition again, and consciously work with the techno-medical bureaucracy. I have to schedule appointments, plan for another surgery, get bloodwork, take time off work, come up with excuses for why I'll be bedridden.

Each organ threatens to undermine our independence.

What is internal alienates, displaces, sends us outside of ourselves. The heart keeps us alive, yet we rarely feel it pumping. We have almost no control over its rhythms. When an organ breaks down, we repair it with instruments and maintain a sense of ourselves as beings with clearly marked borders, even though our insides are penetrated by the outside, even though we only come into ourselves by bringing ourselves out.

Human life is the attempted harmonization of genetic codes and cultural scripts. Character and circumstance join into what we might call fate, or if we permit ourselves to say it, the realization of a divine plan.

What's possible in one era is forgotten in another, and what's impossible at one time becomes a matter of routine in a few years. Within one lifetime, a gulf separates past and future.

Three hundred years ago, I wouldn't have been able to cure my impotence. But three hundred years ago I would've had other lines written for me, other roles, vocations, compensatory beliefs and practices no longer at my disposal.

Western technoscience and medicine have mastered some problems. If my condition is the product of a brute genetic fact, then there can be no other correction than mechanical intervention or, at some point in the future, direct manipulation of the genetic code. There could be no other system for solving this problem other than western instrumental reason modeled on mathematical physics.

Isolation of parts, specialization of knowledge and technique.

The same system that has dominated nature and remade man in the image of a machine, that has thrown darkness on the world of creation in the name of scientific enlightenment, must be credited, at least in my case, with saving me from my own private hell, the torment of arbitrarily imposed impotence, the silence I kept when out in company and the racket of reproaches when shut up inside myself. As for what I do with the time and energy given to me, the value I ascribe to my own life or life in general, the purpose of my strivings, the basis of my hopes and fears, for all this the scientific materialist paradigm offers little to nothing.

A working dick freed me to grasp my spiritual bondage. The promise of mounting pleasure conceals the waywardness of our souls. The pursuit of greater power over matter distracts us from the anguish caused by luxuriating in evil, turning our backs on the truth, refusing to account for our origin and end.

The penis precedes the man, symbolizing and incarnating his excess and lack. Consider his anatomy. The roots of the penis are buried in the body. A great deal of the actual length is hidden and unusable.

Outside the body at the bottom front of the pelvis, a sock of soft tissue hangs, vulnerable and ridiculous. This fluctuating rod is also connected to an extremely delicate nutbag that produces our most vital fluids, the goo of our immortality. A boot to the balls will nearly kill a man; it's enough to flick the sack to bring him to his knees.

The penis is an extremity, an appendage of sorts, but it's not a limb like an arm or a leg. It doesn't respond to conscious direction. Rather the penis dozes and stirs in accordance with unconscious physiological processes and external and uncontrolled stimuli. On top of the unwieldy actions and inconsistent influences, we also have to consider the combined sexual and urinary functions, which for the most part we try to keep separate.

Desire, disgust, shame and guilt concentrated in a piece of flesh that acts through unconscious mechanisms. In its size, shape and activity, the penis is beyond a man's power, but at the same time it forms the subterranean core of his identity. A man bases his value on the functioning of an organ that he must protect, hide and satisfy without injuring or sickening himself.

Genital directives shape body and mind. Man is always outside of himself, even on the inside. Everywhere we look we see a combination of accidents and externalities. Even the conscious experience of initiating a series of actions surges up from invisible depths. Always on the outside, in the middle, caught between before and after, among the facts of our environment, the inscriptions of our instincts and the stories of our culture.

We retain a sense of responsibility, of individuality, ownership of ourselves, even as we move like insects, ants in a colony, even as our parts within parts carry out their own ant-like tasks. In mortal earthly life, innocence is impossible. It's always a question of the degree of guilt, the sharpness of shame's blade, how deeply it cuts into us. How else to explain why, in my earliest prepubescent genital experiences, I felt the need for discretion?

Not yet knowing of sex, yet still somehow acting with an inherited understanding, imprinted instructions, not only to pleasure myself, but to split into at least two selves: the self that exults in this pleasure and the self that recoils from it.

My first prosthesis broke after four years of consistent use. Medical literature states that ninety-five percent of devices still work after ten years. Not only was my initial problem statistically unlikely, but the breakdown of the solution put me in even rarer company.

(That figure of ninety-five percent after ten years likely has something to do with the average age of implanted men, elderly men who probably don't use their device nearly as much as a thirty year-old trying to make up for lost time.)

It happened right before a date. I'd been in the habit of partially inflating my device before I expected to use it. In my car outside her apartment, I pressed on the pump and it flattened, indicating a break. Panic and shame overtook me, a resurgence of that foundational emasculation that had underscored all my efforts throughout my adult life.

Action aids forgetting; memory attacks when movement ceases. The failure of my device summoned twenty years of fumbling, cursing, apologizing. Evenings of fizzled chemistry, whimpering ends, cold retreats. The sense of futility hanging over all my interests, the fog covering all my thoughts.

I was worse off than before my surgery. In the old days I could sometimes get hard for a minute or two, but now I was completely inoperative. Modern medicine has developed techniques for what they call minimally invasive surgery, limiting trauma to the body and speeding up recovery time. Even still, penile implant surgery destroys the natural ability to sustain an erection.

The broken device returned me to my essential self, the self in exile from the empire of permissive individualism, in which each person consumes all available pleasures, and I had to confront, again, my primary fault, as well as the emptiness of the pleasures I'd experienced after my techno-biological upgrade.

Our lives unroll on a strict line. We'd like to convince ourselves that we stand apart from this line, that we can arrange our development, expand and contract time at will, jump forward and backward and accept degrees of maturity and responsibility as we please. Though this power is promoted as completely open-ended, it tends in the direction of the ageing person prolonging or returning to their youth, a youth understood as vibrant, attractive, creative and sexually adventurous. The forty-year-old can live like he's twenty. His options never run out. His freedom to explore his creative and sexual potential hinges on a denial of decay.

An advanced technological society creates categories of time and fabricates stages of life to expand production and consumption. Techniques and systems take hold of the mortal body and enhance its youthful qualities and veil its signs of decline. But it remains true that a thirty year-old man isn't twenty, no matter how much money and effort he puts into preserving or enhancing himself. Those who say, "age is just a number" want to believe their age reduced to a quantity is an arbitrary marker that doesn't correspond to their experience or possibilities.

While the number thirty could be called anything else and represented any other way, the time that has passed, that we have lived, has done its damage, and we feel it and show it despite our desperate attempts to cover it up.

With a new working dick at thirty I could somewhat pretend to be twenty again, in the artificial and historically conditioned sense of a modern twenty year-old, a man unburdened by traditional expectations, free to explore unlimited sensual gratification with an ageless body and a mind purged of neurosis and guilt.

The time I spent as sexually crippled, emotionally ravaged and spiritually anguished couldn't be recovered, only forgotten in a superficial reenactment of an irretrievable period of experimentation and freedom. There I was, sent back to my place on the timeline, having passed through the arena of sanctioned indulgence without being able to indulge. Back to time moving forward with me several steps behind it, using manufactured parts to compensate for an organic insufficiency. Only now, the mechanical parts no longer worked, and the distractions I enjoyed and the powers I'd built on top of those distractions fell apart.

In the first few days after the break I thought about killing myself. My parents have done everything for me; I credit them with keeping me alive, not only in my childhood, but later, when I wanted to die but also knew I could never take my life because of the pain I'd cause them.

It remains nearly impossible to convey the desolation of my spirit, to anyone else and even myself, already looking back now on abbreviated time. Life is so long we lose touch with our own suffering; we read the remnants of our grief like the plaques of historic battlegrounds. Those moments of estrangement, in our intimate loneliness, when all the world zooms out and appears as an expanse of cold space, and we huddle with ourselves, warm ourselves with resentment and self-pity, all that time and all those self-inflicted wounds scab over and slip off.

My attitude was split between wanting to replace my broken device as quickly as possible and reconsidering my need for technologically assisted sex. My dick had never stopped me from finding love. And I didn't feel a strong desire for children. I'd experienced the excitement and boredom of sex, the egoistic thrill of seduction and the tedium of soulless thrusting. Why not celibacy?

I went through with another surgery, and I doubt I ever had a choice. We never know possibility, only what we've done. I emailed a surgeon and scheduled an operation two months away. Those two months were among the most peaceful and studious of my life. I read and wrote and meditated. I barely looked at women.

The second surgery went better than the first. My body was used to the trauma.

Each penile implant surgery increases the risk of infection. It's hard to say how many surgeries I'll need. Sometimes I hope for a decline in desire in old age, but I fear this won't happen, and that I'll play out a laughless comedy of a man still obsessed with his dick as death closes in on him.

ETERNAL SUNSHINE OF THE ISOLATED MIND

BUSY SATURDAY AT THE SHOP. The sound of fifty conversations at once. Dogs barking. The end of my week, two hours left. When I'm done with my shift I go home and stare at the walls, read Houellebecq, pet my cats—the rest of the day is mine.

I don't go to the gym or prepare a nutrient dense meal. I don't read inspirational books or listen to motivational and informative podcasts. My cats yell at me and gallop through the apartment and then they sleep on my belly. I cease thinking.

In the evening I see my girlfriend. We eat dinner and watch a movie. Her work week starts tomorrow. She goes to bed early and I leave with nothing to do. It's my Friday night and I should get out there. But I want to decompose, turn into mulch. Let my body return to organic matter—sprout like an old potato. Worms and flies and beetles and ants taking me apart. Picked clean by buzzards, devoured by wild dogs, stomped by hippos. My rotting head kicked down a hill by inbred children.

Two days off but I need to clean my apartment and get groceries and air up my tires and go to the gym. Visit my parents, drive an hour and a half in my 2005 white Toyota Corolla with the rusted catalytic converter I still haven't replaced and won't ever replace. Work on the short stories and the new novel and these nonfiction pieces and write emails to my virtual friends, the people who've supported my work. Apply to new jobs. I don't want to do any of it.

A warm winter night. Melting snow and the smell of soggy earth, the sidewalks underwater. Stepping onto yards, the sound of sucking mud. Walk with my girlfriend through the neighborhood. We're going to the local arthouse cinema. They're playing *Eternal Sunshine of the Spotless Mind*. I watched it when I was eighteen.

Ten minutes in and I'm thinking Jim Carrey's character is a pussy. Kate Winslett is trying to talk to him on the train and I wonder why he's fumbling so badly. Scoffing at the idea of a shy man attracting a pretty woman because my brain has been fried by the internet. Strangers meeting in public without messaging each other seems impossible.

A passive man is invisible, without presence. He's not in public. He's jacking off to deep sea creature porn, lizards with dicks the size of redwood trees. He's writing lewd messages to twitter personalities, proposing marriage to models on instagram.

The movie came out in 2004. A different universe. Joel and Clementine wouldn't notice each other today because they'd be scrolling through newsfeeds, texting, emailing, their attention divided by a hundred different things.

But in another respect the movie remains relevant. *Eternal Sunshine* depicts a world of isolation. None of the characters have children. There's no sense of a future beyond a single lifetime of work, consumption and episodic romance. With no future and no shared purpose, the past takes on a haunting and monstrous dimension. The painful experiences of yesterday lead nowhere. Memory is a burden to be eliminated through medical technique.

Rather than serving as pieces of a larger whole, the romantic couple is the last outpost of exiles. Two people come together not to build something beyond themselves, but to assuage the spiritual torment of their unmet needs. Deprived of organic social support, the romantic relationship is doomed to a cycle of fascination and boredom. The end is disgust and hatred, or at best a numbed resignation that leaves blank whole stages of life.

The main character of *Eternal Sunshine* is adrift and empty;

he repeatedly says he has nothing to say. But glossed over is the fact that he begins his romance with Clementine while still in a relationship. He lives with another woman named Naomi who never appears. None of his memories involve their breakup.

Even while living with someone, Joel is open to the idea of another partner, a different life, a stranger electrifying him back into a state of heightened awareness. This splitting of the soul between the possible and the actual drains the present of its vitality and all but guarantees the withering of real attachments.

The failure of Joel and Clementine's relationship was prefigured in Joel's disconnection from Naomi. It's not idiosyncratic dysfunction or incompatibility that destroys the couple but rather an environmentally conditioned inability to embed themselves in a greater whole. The social body is sick and can't integrate its parts.

Clementine complains that men see her as a concept. She says she's only a fucked-up girl looking for her own peace of mind. What appears to her as the correct view of herself is a plea to be seen as a different concept, one under her control, which is part of the problem, part of why she also can't commit to anything bigger than the management of her identity and sensations.

One week later. Sunday in a coffee shop where I used to work. Glad I'm not here anymore. Three years ago I was working in the same space with some of the same people working here now. They're wearing masks. They had a sign that said you had to wear a mask to order at the counter. I didn't wear one. Can't tell if they hate me, if they hate the prig who makes them wear a mask or who knows what else. People are unreadable now.

Still need to do the laundry, visit parents, get my tax refund from 2020, do my taxes for 2021. Tried to air up my passenger side tire. Squatting and pressing the hose into the valve, squeezing the lever and getting nothing, pressing and squeezing until I run out of time on the machine.

I drive away hoping the tires will magically fill with air instead of popping on a bend on the interstate between septic trucks and gas tankers and horse trailers. My car with the rusted exhaust system that sounds like an armada of riding lawnmowers, like every other low-class car.

Cold nights in my apartment. Baseboard heater sounds like it's leaking. The next bill is going to bankrupt me. The toilet runs unless I take off the lid and fiddle with one of the pieces and then it won't flush. When I shit I have to take off the lid and tinker with a mechanism until the tank fills with water and then I have to mess with it again to get it to stop running.

Not going to tell my landlord. Last week I thought I lost my keys and all he said was that I'd have to call a locksmith, to get into an apartment with one lock on the main door and a different lock for my apartment. He ignored me until I said I'd found them, and then he said good deal. I'd rather shit in a bucket than interact with him again.

Lease is up in March but I can go month to month now. Blew the apartment deal with my girlfriend. A rare opportunity in flames. We're okay now but it was yet another moment where I failed to do something normal, age appropriate.

A tech guy at the slow shop wants me to write for him. He's got an app that would allow service industry workers to publish their schedules so regular customers can see when they work. I would write newsletters and emails and other annoying bits of information no one ever asks for. He'd pay me more than I'm worth. I'm morally and artistically against this kind of work but I might do it anyway.

If he read what I write online he'd never work with me. If my boss read me he'd fire me. If my landlord read me he'd evict me. If my girlfriend read me she'd break up with me. Good thing no one who could freeze my bank account or blacklist me from an industry or cut off the power to my house ever bothers to check up on what I'm saying. I'm one google search away from getting burned at the stake but there are so many articles and substacks and videos of surfing cats and cartoon wolves jacking off that no one will ever find me.

DIARY OF A SEMI-EMPLOYED MAN

THE MORNING WAS COOL AND GRAY and then it rained. After writing and smoking cigarettes and starting a substack I took a nap. When I woke up the rain had stopped. The air outside was sweaty like a locker room.

Stood on my street and breathed in the steam and walked across the waterlogged ground to my girlfriend's shop. I'm going to write more because I have no excuse now. No excuse not to commit these slow burning days to the page.

I have a paid week off but when it's over there will be no more money. I need to find another job or make money writing.

Better write about abortion. Take a fistful of Adderall suppositories and write about Ukrainian orphans with covid unable to abort their third trimester rape babies. Is that a good thing or a bad thing? Depends on who pays me. *The same people who say my body my choice want to force me to wear a mask. The same people who don't want to wear a mask want to tell me what I can do with my body.*

Women want to fuck without bad things happening to them. Men want it too. Men think it's easier for women to get sex and women think it's easier for men to get everything else. We hate each other. We envy each other's strength and despise each other's weakness.

Part of me wants to limit a woman's sexual power but I also don't blame them for feeling the way they do, their interests align with the modern project. Using technology to conquer nature. Perverting creation to satisfy monstrous whims. I'm no better. It's human nature to subvert our nature, defy the gods. When I say woman should face the consequences of sex, I mean when they're fucking other men, not me.

At least they'll never get what they want and never be happy. Neither will I.

First paid day passing. Can't enjoy it. Can't enjoy anything. I like my apartment but it's expensive.

The apartment I stay in like a guest at a hotel. With its warped hardwood floors, unseen angles and cobwebbed corners. Blinds torn by cats, tattered sunlight on the walls. In the evening I sit in one of two chairs and light a single lamp on the end table. Use the toilet and the sink and the shower. I don't clean until it looks like I'll get an infection from the bathroom.

The tiny kitchen with the built-in cabinets stocked with underused utensils. Stale water in the sink. I pass through my apartment; I pass out of my body. Read in the loveseat while most of my soul sleeps somewhere else.

My bedroom. Light blocking curtains covering wall-spanning windows. Dirty clothes and half-read books. Dust drifting in footsteps and cat gallops.

Dreamless sleep, waking up like a flipped switch. Alienated from my subconscious, locked out of the root cellar of history and myth. As if my unknown life, my shadow, refuses to meet me. Renting an apartment, renting my body and mind, paying for a passage.

The next day I didn't work. A listless afternoon, light rain like whispers in a crowd. Green leaves vivid against the grey. Drank coffee and read a couple chapters. My girlfriend made a quiche. We ate and watched tv. Stayed up late tangled in each other.

Another grey morning, the sun is in the shop for repairs. Going to the gym then working for the carpenter. Caulking walls and stapling insulation. Sheltered from the churn of service. No one asks how I'm doing. By that fact alone I'm doing better than ever.

I lost my job. The café job, both spots, the one in the trendy neighborhood and the one downtown by the convention center. Last week I worked during the firefighters convention. 35,000 people, three days of nonstop drinks.

Firemen are fat louts. Ninety-five percent of the time they're in lounge chairs. They're heroes. Women love them like they tend to love men: as a fantasy, as roles and symbols. Cops, firemen, soldiers. Men in uniform. The meat doesn't matter, it's the starch in the collar.

Someone wrote a bad review, took my picture and said the barista wasn't friendly. People don't want an angry ape steaming their milk. The American public's standard for most things is in the toilet but its standard for friendly service is out beyond the moon. I don't spit in faces or piss in drinks, I greet people, ask what they want and give it to them. It's my reserve. They want a friend for two minutes. Someone who welcomes them. They want a break from their boring routines. I want to hit them over the head with a chair.

American society doesn't just force you to work. That would be normal. It forces you to want to work. Not only to want it, but to show that you want it. They want to know how you're doing, as long as you're doing well.

Where I worked, you could show up late day after day, you could spend half the shift on your phone. You don't need to know how to make good coffee. People don't taste, they drink with their eyes. They consume through the eyes of others.

The only thing you can't do is tarnish the brand. Displease a customer. Bad reviews weigh more than bad days, bad lives. A thousand good reviews shrink before one man who didn't get his balls cradled when he ordered a latte.

Five stars, glittering pictures on instagram. This is what counts. Flesh and blood reality is raw material for the presentation of self. Groaning organs and sour moods downplayed in favor of gliding surfaces. Betrayals and breakdowns papered over to give the idea that everything works as it should.

The owner of the shop said I could stay at the downtown spot in the drab office building but not the trendy location where women with hats take pictures of their drinks. He offered to pay me for my last scheduled week. A strongly suggested resignation. Like I'm a CEO or a politician with a trail of treacherous hookers behind him. Stepping down from my position on the bottom to save the image of a café.

What a relief. Getting fired is my highest promotion. I'm at home when I move on. Jobs, apartments, girlfriends, interests, everything streaming past and disintegrating except some blackened pit in my stomach, some indigestible kernel of my character. Everything changes except me.

A paid week off without working. Except I'll be scrambling to find a new job, earn a living. At least I'm still working for the carpenter. A few hours here and there. It helps. Somewhere down the line he'll be able to pay me more, give me more hours. When his workshop is finished we can build four thousand dollar oak tables for rich widows in cottage homes.

When I qualify as a journeyman carpenter I'll be worth at least thirty-one dollars an hour. I need something else to fill the gaps in the meantime. Service industry jobs are easy to get but

I should be kept away from the public. Hidden like a burn victim.

Tuesday morning, the first free one in a long time. Thunder and rain. Then the rain stops. Navy blue clouds thick like canvas, storm winds waving the freshly green leaves. Beaming white magnolias. The smell of spring, blooming flowers, damp dirt. Sweet bird songs, the swelling earth.

Flashes of memory, last spring and the hellish summer that followed. When I worked two jobs and chased a woman who didn't want me. I'm with her now and she says everything is fine. We spend afternoons and evenings together. We make love almost every night. Most of the time it feels perfect but then I remember the things she said last year, what she did. A thousand loving moments die before a cruel sentence, a thoughtless act.

I can forget everything but what I need to forget to be happy. She wants me now but I still wonder why she didn't back then. I'm always the same man. What changed in her, what changed in us?

From a logical standpoint, I can understand. People make mistakes, they fail to see what's important, they learn. But the objective reality of what we've done weighs more on others than it weighs on ourselves. We have our subjective rationalizations, which are easy to carry, and others have the fact that we hurt them, which is crushing.

Still, there's some hope. Flickering gratitude for what I have now, what we have. I want to share the best of what's left of us.

Now that I don't have a job, I'll be working harder.

WHEN LOST TIME HUNTS YOU DOWN

WORKING PART-TIME for a carpenter now. An old grizzled man who comes into my girlfriend's coffee shop. Looks like a steampunk elf. Bowler hat and vest, long ratty beard. Sooty skin and rotting gums, chain smokes black American spirits.

When I finish at the café I help him fix up a studio where he'll teach me to make custom furniture. Hours of prying boards out of walls, putting up insulation, moving heavy tools and hauling lumber. He pays me cash at the end of the day. If anyone at the IRS is reading, of course I promptly record my earnings.

The work clears my head. Helps me forget the world. In a gutted house with missing floorboards, prying and hammering and sawing and stapling, breathing in the dust of vermin turds. It feels right. I want glass and asbestos in my lungs, splinters in my hands.

The first day I gashed my left hand on a rusty nail. Can't tell if it's gangrenous. Might have lockjaw. My dream of being an itinerant day laborer has come true. Work until my body aches and then I take some of the cash and spend it on beer and sandwiches. The only thing missing is sleeping on a bed of straw in a barn.

My genes weren't meant for a life of inscription. A cerebral vocation. Laptop labor. Cultivating my image, managing relationships, driving sales, doing numbers. The aspirations of an artist were grafted onto me through an accident of time and place. Intellectual interests are parasitic aliens sucking the blood of a dumb toiling animal.

I shouldn't have the vocabulary for exploring my feelings. I should grunt and spit and curse, wipe my brow and sit in silence. But I bring the depths to the shallows and trivialize them. In the confessional age, the fate of truth is trivia.

When I tell women about the carpentry apprenticeship their eyes flush with excitement. Liberal urban women who talk about toxic masculinity. They say you should go to therapy but their loins explode at the thought of you swinging a sledgehammer.

My girlfriend took a trip to France. Her second in a year. Staying with her gay best friend in Paris for eleven days. I know what the internet thinks about that. I'm a cuck.

Ten years ago I dated a young woman in the comparative literature department at Indiana University. She was twenty-one. I was twenty-five, an old undergraduate, having gone back to school after five years of playing music, working in kitchens and doing mushrooms.

We met in a literature course. Something about the literature of empire. Coetzee and Camões. I don't remember much about the books but I remember her. Blonde hair, blue eyes and a smile from a toothpaste commercial. We made each other laugh.

Then she went to study abroad in France. Aix-en-Provence. We planned to stay together. Talk on skype. I struggled to suppress my jealousy. My brain overflowed with agonizing scenes. Languorous afternoons in seaside apartments, filthy French pubes in her face. Gentle winds rustling the drapes, lapping waves and squeaking beds.

(I imagined then, and still imagine to this day, that for a woman, casual sex is on the same plane of pleasure, frivolity and inconsequence as ordering an interesting croissant at a bistro. While, for a man, pursuing sex is like hunting a deer. Men and women are fated to misunderstand each other.)

She was young, bookish but radiant. She still had much to "experience". So I couldn't help but imagine. We talked the first two or three days after she left. Then she cut me off.

I moved into my friend's place and tried to distract myself. For two or three months I'd wake up angry, adrenalized like I'd been fighting a badger in my sleep.

(I'd been reading Proust's In Search of Lost Time, *and I'd frequently reflect on the inevitability of betrayal, the impossibility of knowing someone. To my mind at the time, the lover always harbors someone else within them, someone you'll never touch, but will glimpse when they turn against you.)*

She's not a bad person; I had no chance. The timing worked against me. Like it does with most of us. Love isn't absent; it's late or early. It doesn't sidestep you; it flays your ass on the way to someone else.

I didn't talk to her for six months. When she was over there she met the man she would go on to marry. Maybe there weren't unwashed orgies. Hard to say if it feels better to be left for a future husband or a score of anonymous lovers.

I wrote an album about her dumping me. Shoegaze, dreampop, two guitars and vocals. We played a few shows, recorded a cassette. People liked it. I wish I could say the creation of art consoles a man for lost love, but I've never believed it.

Sometimes I think I'd rather have been a placid moron with a wife and children. Breaking rocks all day and swilling whisky, a flicker of despair snuffed out by a tv.

Woke up at three this morning even though I went to bed beyond exhausted. After spending my day off working for the carpenter. Must've been disturbed by some blue light or wifi rays or a microwave running in my neighbor's kitchen. Now my testosterone will crash and I'll get fat. Jerk off to porn and send money to camgirls.

I have to calibrate every detail of my life to maximize testosterone production so I can send manly emails and write badass tweets and have sex with women who'll forget who I am in a month. Repeat this until I'm eighty. The pickup artists said it's better to enjoy the memories of heated trysts on your deathbed than review decades of marital drudgery. But I can't even remember sex from last summer.

I want to forget it all. Chasing after a persona. Neurotically fixating on the minutiae of my physical and mental functioning, the microscopic monsters in my environment. Instead, I want to chug tap water and bathe in canola oil and get four hours of sleep a night on sheets of quilted receipt paper. Marry some ill-mannered woman and never think about what she did or might do when I'm not around. Impregnate her and raise a bunch of robust Cro-Magnons.

She's still in France. We talked on the phone and she says she wants to go again in August. I won't have my passport in time. I had to get a new birth certificate because I lost my old one (without a birth certificate, it isn't certain I was ever born).

No passport because I have no taste for travel. No inclination for elegance, decoration, fun, frivolity, the charms of life. Left to myself I'd live in a rusted out Buick. But my girlfriend wants to go everywhere and experience everything, and because I have nowhere to go, I'm along for the ride.

My car wouldn't start when I tried to leave the carpenter's studio. He gave me a jump and I drove to my place. The next morning the car wouldn't start so I rode my vintage Schwinn Suburban to work. It's only three miles but the bike chain is rusted and the gears slip. No time to deal with the battery; after work I rode to the carpenter's and worked for him into the evening.

The next day I biked to work again. Early spring weather, still freezing cold, bursts of chilling wind. In the afternoon my manager came to my place and gave me a jump and I took the car to AutoZone, where I've been told they'll replace the battery. I don't have any tools at my apartment.

When I got to AutoZone the woman told me she can't replace the battery because there are only two employees in the store and she can't leave the other one alone. The store is on crackhead row; they have to protect themselves from the threat of a tweaker smashing their skulls in with a monkey wrench. The woman said there's another shop a couple miles down the street and they might have more employees.

I went to my car and turned the key in the ignition. Miraculously it started, sputtering and coughing. Down the road to the next AutoZone, where a woman told me she can't help until a coworker comes back in an hour. I left the car and wandered the dreary streets and smoked cigarettes in the cold wind. Grey skies and a colorless landscape. The blight of commercial real estate. Check- cashing stores, liquor stores, a CVS and grimy parking lots. Roaring traffic, dimwits driving from their shit jobs to their shit homes, junkies in junk cars much like mine.

Talked to one of my internet friends, a distinguished poet, a smart person. When I filled her in on my personal problems she said I was an insane idiot. Back at the AutoZone and a different cast of employees. Some fifteen year-old with acne and a sideways baseball cap said he couldn't leave the store to change the battery. I bought a new battery and said I need a jump to get out of the parking lot. He left the store to jump my car.

Finally, I drove back to my apartment and called a former coworker who brought a wrench and we changed the battery. Now I can drive to work and home again and pick up my girlfriend from the airport, unless a tire pops or the engine falls out or the brakes fail or the belt breaks or the starter stops working or she comes back with a European husband. Everything around your full-time job is a full-time job and everything you want to keep is breaking apart.

Made it to the weekend. Time to take a breath. Slept like a man submerged in the ocean, woke up weightless, refreshed. Drinking espresso outside a café in the glorious morning light. A little finch pecks at a muffin. A hobo shuffles by, his pants sagging, his buttcheeks showing. Right now everything is fine. I'm invulnerable, I don't exist in the realm of past and future, of wistful memory and dreadful expectation.

I'm getting closer to rudimentary competence. Now I can change a car battery. Soon I'll be able to build a chair.

DISPATCH FROM DETROIT

Calling for the dismantling of a system *is a defense mechanism of a system, a placating ritual and a show of group membership. Mass corporations devote considerable resources and labor to signaling agreement with deconstructive agendas, marginal identities and destructive impulses as they tighten their grip on markets and pump out more products, creating an impression of social momentum while fueling consumerist habits that prevent people from establishing autonomous local economies and distinctive communities and cultures.*

Mass institutions further the dependence on large-scale economic and social structures even as they condemn systemic forces. When official organizations split themselves off from shadowy background powers and claim to oppose their own invisible influence by projecting it as systemic oppression, they legitimize a paranoid and conspiratorial mindset that consumes itself in hysterical interpretation.

The beauty of some days precludes all effort. On Sunday I needed to clean and do laundry before a trip to Detroit. Nothing happened in the morning. I was transparent, thoughtless.

On Saturday I tore up a plywood floor. Sawed it into sections and then pried them away from the base, the sound of cheap wood cracking over the radio.

Larry the carpenter cut wood for pieces of a storefront. We worked in his studio. Caulking holes in the walls for two hours straight, I realized I hadn't had one conversation, hadn't been interrupted once. Your job in the service industry is to be overjoyed about random idiots bothering you.

Some days are destined for indolence. They unroll like a lazily kicked rug. Work stays with you when you're not working. Feeds on your joints like a chronic illness. Before, in the coffee shop, there were people I didn't want to see. People I had to treat like friends instead of giant pests that should be beaten with a shovel.

The work you've done adds up, in damage to your body and

soul, but you start each day at zero. Doing what you did again. Something is subtracted from you, but you have to act as if you're building yourself up.

Sunday afternoon my girlfriend and I drove to Detroit. One of her favorite musicians was playing a show.

No air conditioning in the car. But the weather was mild, the skies overcast. We drove through the flatlands of Indiana, soybean fields dotted with silos and farmhouses. We stayed at an Air B & B run by a middle-aged woman. A private bedroom in an historic apartment with brick siding and walls like paper. Doors that whined like fighter jets.

When I think of Air B & B's, I think of a person renting out space, managing it from elsewhere. We stayed at this woman's apartment and she was there the entire time. Her bedroom was two feet away from ours. We lived with her.

Through two closed doors I could hear her clearing her throat. I could hear my pulse, hear thoughts rustling like centipedes in dry leaves. Our designated bathroom was between the two bedrooms. The most nerve-wracking shits of my life. Tried to make as little noise as possible, let everything slip out. It was thunder in a valley, it filled the rooms and shook portraits on the walls.

The city felt abandoned, like an old model in a basement. On Monday the weather was pleasant. We wandered Mexican town and Corktown. Many shops and cafes were closed. Downtown had no traffic. People here and there walked to their office jobs.

Shops without crowds, without lines. But the same aesthetic as Indy, as everywhere else. Minimalist interiors, black and white. Repurposed industrial space. The same spotify playlists, the same brunch menus. Tattooed servers and baristas and line cooks, frustrated artists, musicians. People with nothing else to do. They were promised the world, told they could do whatever they wanted and then given a spatula.

Monday night at El Club. My girlfriend had a good time, and I was happy to be there with her, but I'd be fine with never going to a live music performance for the rest of my life. The first crowd I encountered in the city. Pressed against fat sweating strangers. I have the temperament of a one hundred and ten year-old man. The music was too loud and I was tired.

Tuesday we walked the sleepy streets downtown. Should've been a bustling morning in the motor city but it was like an afternoon in an Italian village. We sat outside a café, leaned against the shaded walls, spoke now and then. She took pictures of me, of us. She asked why I don't take pictures.

I couldn't tell her why. I should've laid a lecture on her. Referenced Roland Barthes and Walter Benjamin. But I'm not always sharp and I don't always want to explain myself.

I wanted to say it's because I already live as if I'm flipping through a photo album. The present comes to me as a memory from the future. I know what's in front of me will be gone, or rather, that it never arrives outside my anticipation and recall, and that a picture is only a symbol, a painful reminder that parts of us were never there, have never been present.

Some people take pictures, they hold themselves at a distance from what they experience to carve out a piece for the future. I do the same thing, but instead of pressing a button, I write what I see and think and feel, hours and days after events. Either way there's an exchange: immediacy for permanence, presence for memory, life for art. To write is to remove yourself from time. To see yourself out.

It was early afternoon, the sun burned in the cloudless sky. Before we left we stopped at a food truck by the interstate on the Canadian border. A gravel lot shimmering in the heat. At a plastic table we loaded up on greasy sandwiches and garlic fries and looked forward to going home.

Drove back with no air conditioning, eighty-five degrees in the car. Sun lit us up like an angry interrogator. The sky was blazing, white as a desert at noon. I have to give us credit: we didn't murder each other. We didn't fight at all.

The next day I went to work. Nine hours building a temporary wall in an antique shop, then redoing the façade. A world of exact measurements, straight lines. Unlike my preferred realm of letters, interpretation, ambiguity.

If I write poorly, I'm only wasting time, and I might annoy someone who reads me. If I mess up on a construction job, I could cut my foot off.

❦

Now that I'm not opening a café, my mornings don't start until much later. I'm not stumbling out the door at five with dried mucus in my eyes. A fantasy life, impossible to maintain. When you work you dream of not working and when you don't work you have to think about finding work again.

That carpentry job on the antique shop façade is beyond my abilities. I can't help Larry. He said he'll let me know when I could work for him again. Could be days, a week or more. I suspect he thinks I'm retarded, liable to shoot myself in the groin with a nail gun.

The last day I worked I had to chase down a black woman who'd stolen the shop owner's wallet. Larry told me to go get her. I took off my tool belt and sprinted down the sidewalk. She had two or three blocks on me but I caught up to her and grabbed her shoulder and ripped the wallet out of her hands.

I was on 10th street by a gas station. I had an audience. A fat black woman wearing a shower cap on her head and a shower curtain for a dress called me a cracker and said she was going to kill me. Someone would kill me; she'd make sure of it. I doubt she could do it on her own but she probably knows more than one man with automatic pistols.

I can't measure or cut a straight line through a ceiling but I can chase black women down in front of bus stops and gas stations and front porches, in view of people looking at me like I'm wearing a white hood on horseback. Like I'm not a day laborer with two figures in his bank account.

I'm lucky I wasn't lured into a trap. I could've followed the woman around the corner to a gang of men with crowbars. Who would've helped me then? Who would've thrown down their toolbelt or microwave meal or their phone and rushed to my defense?

What about the cops, doing slow laps around 10th and Washington St? They pull me over for having a taillight out or not wearing my seatbelt but I could see them rolling by as a crew of promising young men beat me with bike locks and garden hoses.

Everyone thanked me for risking my life. I wonder if they'd expect me to save the day if the thief had been a 6'5 300-pound man rather than a woman whittled down to chicken bones.

You're not supposed to do anything on your own. Not

supposed to fight back, stand up for yourself or those around you. Too risky, you never know. Every person on the street could stab or shoot you. Their friends could kick your head until you black out, their pack of pit bulls could rip your lips off. They might run you over with a truck.

When in doubt, give up your wallet, your tools, your clothes, your butthole. Call the authorities; when those authorities ignore you, call some other authorities. File a complaint with the committee that oversees the police department, submit a formal request for an investigation. When the city fails, go to the state. When the state fails, go to the national government. Try the United Nations.

A low trust society gives rise to greater complexity, higher security costs and a draining sense of unease. Middlemen shoehorning themselves in the middle of the middle of the middle of emotionally taxing interactions. Increasing atomization results in increasing litigation, multiplication of laws, rules, processes, more virtual confrontations and continued withdrawal from the public sphere. On the internet people fight like baboons. In real life they shuffle between brew bars and coffee shops, hoping to avoid conflict.

Men of even temperaments are encouraged to suppress themselves, which leaves the field open to the vicious. The elite program is to disempower communal standard bearers and kindle the fires of volatile outcasts. The breakdown of small-scale social order then invites bureaucratic intervention.

We see men with the cosmetics of Viking warriors and the hearts of court eunuchs. There seems to be an alien force at work in the world today, always targeting the center, mining the middle ground, vaporizing the solid and the stable, leaving only the dangerous extremes and exceptions.

If fascism has reemerged as a threat to progress, or as a counter to a corrupt system, it's because our social and economic conditions appear especially unstable. Isolated and vulnerable people indulge in violent fantasies of political revolution as their lives quietly float off course. On the left, the hysterical fear of fascism is an expression of a masochistic desire for punishment, and on the right, the appeal of fascism lies in nihilistic destruction parading as imposition of order.

The individual isn't the building block of society, but its detritus. Scratch the surface of any fascist movement, its image of upright men leading families, and you find homosexual drug addicts desperate for a thrill. Behind a poster of beauty, health and vitality lurks a stifled soul longing for annihilation. Extreme phenomena capture the popular imagination and dominate political discourse because there is no longer any moderate or cohesive social body to stabilize frustrated urges, nor is there a religious or spiritual framework for sublimating dark drives.

Wake up in my dank apartment, cats scampering about. Drink coffee, smoke, walk around the block. Try to enjoy the cool mornings, the soft light on the leaves. The still surroundings. In the windless air, the trees stand like exhibits in a museum. I'm thinking about money.

The things you want to do make up one percent of life. If you could do them all the time, you'd want to do something else. No wonder we tend to believe in an afterlife.

COLD FRENCH FRIES

I SPENT THE GREATER PART of my first paycheck in a month on a plane ticket to New York City. Maybe I'll be able to pay my rent. Maybe I'll die on a park bench in a puddle of my own flesh.

Indiana, the middle of June. The heat of early summer. Air like a mausoleum. So hot you sweat standing in the shade. Stagnant economy of an equatorial nation heat. Import a slave class so you can sleep all afternoon on the porch heat. My mind isn't working. Can't think, can't write. Need bare-breasted native women to fan me with palm fronds.

Central Indiana, no ocean breeze, no waves in the winds. Grass beaten brown by the sun. Outside the city, the fields roll on forever.

I don't want to do anything but sit naked under a tree and eat mangoes and make love to my girlfriend. But I have to go to my part-time job and find a full-time job, be a good friend and son, call my parents, read classic works of literature, entertain people on the internet.

Show up for job interviews where I know they know I don't want to work there. Bad forced dates where we both squirm in our chairs and eye the exit. I'm a one-hundred-year-old man interviewing at places where twenty-year-olds work for weed money.

Employers need workers and workers need jobs. Workers want more money than what employers want to pay. Everyone looking for love, money, affirmation, security, good help, identity, belonging; but at a lower cost for less effort. Each person a tool for everyone else. Insist on more for less long enough and you end up with nothing.

Emails from indeed pouring into my inbox. Jorge Ponce thinks my fifteen years of experience in cafes would make me a good fit for his warehouse supervisor position. There's no Jorge Ponce and there's no warehouse. The warehouse is a pile of shattered cinderblocks and rusted steel drums crawling with possums. Jorge Ponce is an artificial intelligence composite of two Mexican men and an Indian woman, a call center cyborg.

Right now I'm working three nights a week in a New American restaurant that serves experimental cheeseburgers and monopoly man hot dogs. Four hundred-dollar checks, a tasting menu with wine pairings. Hosting, the easiest job in the business, except everyone hates you.

In the service industry, you're always pissing someone off. The guests want to sit anywhere but where you seat them. The servers want you to seat more people faster when you slow down and they want you to seat fewer people at a slower pace when you speed up. Someone's always in the wrong section. They wait until you seat them and fill their water; they blow their nose on their napkins and pick their ears with the knives and then decide they want to sit outside.

Whatever you're doing, someone wants you to do something else. When you're polishing silverware you should be refilling water. When you refill water they run out of silverware. A table needs bussing so you grab a rag and wring it and ten people walk through the door. A full party never shows up together. You seat three of them, one more on the way, he's running ten minutes late. Twenty minutes late, he's stuck in traffic, he's in a forty-car pile up, his lower half is crushed under the steering wheel, he's going to lose his legs, he'll be there in an hour.

Forget shift breaks, sitting down and eating a meal. You cram a few cold french fries in your mouth by the dishwasher; thirty seconds away from the action feels like dereliction of duty, homicidal negligence. Before you can choke down the first bite of a crab cake, a server busts through the door balancing a load of dishes and gives you an ambiguously hateful look.

Was it you or another server? Was it a customer or did they just break up with their boyfriend? The ex they want back isn't texting them, the ex they don't want back is texting them ten times a day. Student loan bill is due, they're out of coke, forgot to take their meds, had a fight with their dad. You never know if your coworker wants to get a beer with you, have sex with you or set you on fire. Or all three.

A coworker mocks another coworker, you let a scornful laugh bubble out like a bored aristocrat. Ten minutes later they're sarcastically quipping about you to the person they ridiculed. The evening deepens, you grow tired, irritable. You drink a shift beer. Sneak a shot of tequila or two. One of those chummy dimwits who dines at a place three nights a week but who everyone mildly resents buys a round of drinks for the waitstaff.

You get drunk but you can't enjoy it. Have to focus; walk between narrow aisles without elbowing people in the head, knit your brow to avoid crashing into a high-top table holding glasses of red wine and pig taint with revolutionary mustard. Can't get caught with your eyes lingering on a low-cut blouse. When the restaurant closes you're hungover. Too old to go out after work but you can't fall asleep either.

One more set of coworkers and customers, sprinting through an accelerated acquaintanceship program. Every interaction mediated by money. The market bearing down on us, forcing us into these ill-fitting roles but we have to act like friends, neighbors, members of a community. Doing what we love.

The leftist concept of emotional labor used to describe how service jobs require a performance of happiness and camaraderie. Now the idea is cited in a petulant demand to be paid for listening to your friends and family. Economic thinking has seeped into every domain, corrupted all relationships. We feel pressured to treat coworkers like friends and feel entitled to treat friends and family like clients. A warm smiling face for bloodless transactions and a self-interested logic applied to the most intimate bonds.

The day was hot and then the heat dropped off. Evening reprieve. Lounging outside my girlfriend's apartment building, facing the chain-link fence woven with leaves. Sky flushed pink. On the other side of the fence, a high school campus. Stately trees shading the gentle hills. I don't know if time is passing or I'm passing out of time.

Falling night, the end of another day. A dreamless sleep, waking up to morning light colored like a stone. Good to have someone there. Lying in bed doesn't feel as lazy when someone dozes by your side. Scattered words, yawns, free association. Time hasn't yet taken off.

New York City in August. Brooklyn. Going to a reading with my internet literature friends. The internet has ruined my life and made the ruins inhabitable.

Driving down Washington St. Four lanes bordered by strip malls and government assisted housing. Crackwhores hobbling down the sidewalks. Men with shifty eyes and sagging sweatpants standing in gas station parking lots.

The car in front of me swerves to avoid a detached hubcap. I hit it head on and it shatters under my car. A flapping sound,

I think a tire has popped. When I pull over I see the tire is fine but the hubcap has broken the rusted splash guard. It hangs lower now and scrapes the ground when I turn or back up.

The hot water in my apartment went out. The landlord said the building needs a new commercial grade heater. Supply chain issues, it's taking longer than usual to arrive. Five or six days of cold showers.

According to the internet, these cold showers should improve my mood, reduce anxiety and transform me into a Navy Seal. Like all supplements and motivational tweet threads and stirring youtube speeches about living with urgency and unlocking your power, cold showers do nothing. I've tried every breathing method, meditation program, organizational approach, time management trick. I've read the stoics and the skeptics and the moralists and the church fathers; the only things that help are drugs and money.

If you don't know anyone who wants to waste hundreds of thousands of dollars on you and you're not taking steroids and amphetamines, you can spend all your days trying different brands of fish oil and mushroom tea and new workout routines and none of it will matter.

Last weekend. A flea market in my neighborhood. People from all over the city setting up tables of old clothes, books, dvd's. Lawns crowded with dusty furniture and bad paintings. Food trucks selling tacos and funnel cakes and brisket. My quiet neighborhood overrun with well-to do antique seekers and hillbilly junk hunters.

I sat in the sun all day Saturday and sold two vintage bicycles to pay rent. Haven't done any more carpentry. Larry thinks I'm an incompetent pussy. I cut a line through his ceiling that was 1/36th of an inch off center and now he's going to have to tear his studio down. My hand shaking for a quarter of a second cost him his life savings.

You should learn a trade, learn to work with your hands, earn your bread by the sweat of your brow, they say. It sounds like the right thing to do. Especially with everyone zoom calling, writing emails and taking three-hour coffee breaks, administrating the administrative tasks of other administrators, scheduling meetings about meetings about how to schedule meetings.

With all the consultants and contractors, the brand experience managers, the counselors and coaches and advisers and experts, the community organizers and inclusivity engineers and diversity technicians and advertisers and outreachers, the YouTube and TikTok stars and influencers and money making schemes, the financial system speculators, the new age wishful thinking quantum field manipulators, the drug pushers and psychiatric charlatans and self-care swindlers, the simulation spinners, the fake work funding fake lifestyle digital self-promotion vaudevillian tap dancing acts, we need real men returning to real manly work, driving spikes and balancing on steel beams.

But I'm almost thirty-six years old and I spent my teenage years playing the classical guitar, my early twenties doing mushrooms and reading Schopenhauer and Proust. My late twenties working in coffee shops and writing a blog. I have a degree in comparative literature and I cry when I listen to Bach harpsichord concertos. I look like a man who should be able to raise a barn or work in a steel mill or smash a barstool over a biker's head but I would rather read literature by gay Frenchmen and depressed Germans.

The truth is that I suck at everything involving my hands except fretting a guitar or tapping on a MacBook Pro. When I try to make money with a trade I end up wrenching wrongly as an old man with rotting teeth calls me an idiot.

I've applied to every office job and every administrative assistant position in the city. Had one interview in what might as well have been a computer-generated office building in some randomized industrial park surrounded by chain link fences and sprawling parking lots, where a fidgety man in a polo shirt and a baseball cap and cargo shorts said he'd get back to me soon. He got back to me never. For all I know the business has been bulldozed to make way for a Denny's.

I'm told I'm well-spoken but I must smell like a sewer pipe clogged with dead bodies or my resume reads like I'm a syphilitic horse thief because I'm passed over for white collar work a monkey could perform. I'm in competition with three-hundred-pound women with associate degrees from Johnsonville Tech who watch *The Bachelor* and post glittering gifs on facebook and I lose every time.

There's only one industry desperate enough to take a chance on me, and that's the service industry, where the norm is twenty year-old part time college students not showing up for work because they're drunk from the night before.

Back to work in a restaurant where a veneer of sophistication covers broken systems and crumbling personal lives. The only kind of place that'll give me a job is a week away from a television food critic's five-star review and two weeks from going bankrupt or burning down in a kitchen staff revolt.

I'm hosting part time at another nice restaurant. Just down the road from my neighborhood. I didn't even fill out an application or send them a resume. For all they know I rob jewelry stores and molest children.

Evening hours, working when I have nothing left. My shifts start at five. I'm ready to sleep but instead I'll greet people with the enthusiasm of a game show host. Guide them to their tables, give them the a la carte menu, the tasting menu and a wine list. Fill their water glasses, buss tables, polish silverware. I need a second-grade education to do this job, but also the temperament of someone who doesn't fantasize about running people over with a riding lawn mower.

Rereading *The Elementary Particles*. I read depressing realist literature to escape from a depressing reality. A novel about half-brothers, fragments of a broken family. The two sides of modern society: scientific materialism and cynical hedonism.

One brother a scientist, the other an English teacher. One empty of erotic longing, the other consumed by it. Two halves estranged from each other and themselves. Shaped by their time yet disconnected from it.

Sexual liberation ends in bondage to impulse, imprisonment within a degrading body. Dread and regret rise with the breakdown of organs.

When I was in my twenties my dad tried to give me advice.

He said *don't let your dick control your life.* I thought *what else is there?*.

No one taught me my only purpose was to unload my balls. But I felt the truth in the hollow of my chest after every ejaculation. God is dead and science is dull. The machines have been built, the great works written, the major wars fought. Nothing left to do but get off.

Without a religious order to focus our aims upward, the lower urges dominate. The purpose of external authority is to suppress the tyrants within. Every man is composed of little Caligulas. My dick doesn't care about my happiness. Or the happiness of anyone else.

We tell ourselves the sex drive is biological. The opposite is true. The drive is spiritual, malevolent. You're not swiping on tinder until your thumbprints wear off because of a primal desire to impregnate. You're not forcing stilted conversation on a stranger with big tits at the bar because you envision your offspring tilling the fields.

Contemporary desire is anti-social, thanatological. Body parts are caught in a web of historical and technological influences. Reproductive organs become charged with the energy of their social environment. Pursuit of sex for its own sake increases isolation. It reinforces the separation of the ego, the loneliness of the heart, the covetousness of the soul.

Freedom from religion, God, tradition. Paternal authority, family. This freedom is abandonment to advertising, corporate pressure, the mass mind. No one is ever free, it's only a question of who or what is the master.

Without God, how can life be anything more than a senseless struggle? Each man your competitor or an accomplice to a crime. True joy comes from beyond the earth, outside the ravages of space and time. Still I cling to my mortal life like I would a streetlight in a tornado.

❧

Last night I worked at the restaurant. Today I'm waiting on a text from Larry the carpenter. I'm going into his studio to tear down the ceiling and rip down more walls. Inhale plaster, drink the dust, step on nails, hammer my fingers, caulk my peehole.

I guess I'm not as inept as I thought, or Larry is that desperate for help. After working on that antique shop façade, that day when I tackled a mentally ill black woman in front of a crowd of angry idlers, I haven't done any carpentry work. Haven't reached out either. Tired of begging people to let me work for them. Tired of trying to get everyone's attention.

It's no wonder people tap out and jerk off all day. I can't bring myself to do it but I also have this masochistic motor running all the time that keeps me working at menial jobs and obscure projects as punishment for the crime of being born. Digging holes in fields of clay with a plastic spoon under the nuclear sun. The harder and less fulfilling the job the more gratifying.

Yesterday I did five hundred pushups because a man on the internet said I was mentally weak if I couldn't do it. A digital image questioned my manhood and had me pushing against the floor for an hour.

But my fortitude never translates into a practical venture. All this toughness and focus and I channel it into doing thousands of naked jumping jacks in my living room, reading

Nietzsche and Hegel until I can't see straight, until I don't know what century I'm in.

I'm in my backyard wearing a stahlhelm, doing one-armed pullups from sparking power lines, reciting Lord Byron and rehearsing arguments for why individualism shreds the social fabric. Never building a business, learning a trade, figuring out how to scam the system. Volunteering in a nursing home, feeding orphans of war. Meeting the right people. Playing the stock market, investing, diversifying portfolios. Designing apps, new ponzi schemes. Collecting coupons. No savviness in the ways of life. Just a maniacal will to learn lute suites on the guitar and read about the reformation.

Interviewed for a moving and junk hauling company last week. I went to the opposite side of the city to the wrong location. The address on google maps was outdated. When I found the right place and walked through the door of the office, three dogs ran out into the parking lot.

The interviewer was younger than me and wouldn't make eye contact. He felt the need to say a few things about himself. *I'm an easy guy to get along with until you piss me off.* Which either means nothing or that he has corpses buried under broken furniture. *I have a personality with vestiges of old-school working-class masculinity, but when you touch my emotional tripwires I smash a set of dinner plates.*

The company can't find help. No one who applies has a driver's license. I have a license so I can start out as a captain and drive a whale penis of a truck down narrow streets, blasting side view mirrors and busting street signs and hydrants and running into those green electrical boxes. I'm immediately eligible for a promotion to be the guy everyone hates when they encounter him on the road.

To get a basic office job I'd need to know the president of the United States and have letters of recommendation from the Bilderberg group. The jobs where I can get interviews, they're pleasantly surprised I have no felonies on my record. For the kind of job I'd like, I'd need a doctoral degree from Harvard and a deal with Satan. For the kind of job that's available, they're eager to hire me on the spot because I have no head wounds.

SERVING THE CHILDREN OF MEN

NEW CAFÉ OPENED LAST WEEK. Simple design, black and white color scheme. An old mechanic's garage next to a busy bike trail in the middle of a hip neighborhood. We serve breakfast and lunch. Fancy chicken salad, long johns and lattes.

No mechanics now, just high school girls working for crop-top money and one ageing artist struggling to pay the rent. From skilled labor to the topsy-turvy service economy. A consumption carnival. I'm a toothless carney, cranking the lever on rides. Smoking meth in the port-a-potty and leering at teenage girls.

Apparently, no one has money and everything is more expensive. The pandemic destroyed the economy. World leaders plan to put us in dresser drawers and feed us bug pellets. Industries were flipped upside down, pockets emptied of lunch money. Stores were closed.

Apparently, no one has children anymore. No one gets married. Every thirty year-old man lives with ten roommates and jacks off ten times a day in the linen closet. Women build electric fences around their pussies. Men cut off their nuts with garden shears.

The fertility crisis, the climate disaster, the recession, the depression. Civilization about to collapse, some guy on twitter with a camo baseball cap saying you really don't know how bad it's going to get in the next two years.

But when I work in these cafes and restaurants, I see men and women younger than me with children. Parents spending money on breakfast sandwiches, apple fritters, dirty chais, lamb burgers with sauces whose names I can't pronounce. No one in the western world has money or children except for every single person that comes into the places I work.

I see birthdays and wedding anniversaries. Fathers fattening their children with fried cream filling. Husbands and wives treating themselves to a tasting menu.

On the internet I hear I'm going down the abyssal toilet with all the other loners. At work I serve married couples and children and family friends. Discourse and reality are pulled apart and snap like a wishbone at Thanksgiving.

Last week at the restaurant I seated a twelve top. A surprise birthday party for a married man turning thirty-one years old, surrounded by friends who planned the event. Another friend called the night before and bought the table a hundred-dollar bottle of prosecco.

A man five years younger than me with a pretty wife, enjoying fine dining on his birthday. When I filled their glasses I heard them talking about tv and rock climbing. I like to think I'm better but when I'm at home with my family I talk about tv and lifting weights.

I want to think his wife cheats on him with two of his buddies at the table, with her boss or manager, her physical trainer, her friend from college, some guy who messaged her on Instagram. He cheats on her with two of her friends. They're in debt, trading their children's future for thinly sliced ribeyes. But maybe not.

Maybe not everyone has fifteen internet affairs and huffs felt pen fumes before picking up their kids from karate. Maybe not everyone dreams of another life for the purpose of torturing themselves. But I can't be alone: people are so wretched they fantasize about failing. A man who sleeps on silk sheets wonders if he missed out on the comforts of a dumpster.

I had dinner with my publisher's father. A seventy year-old man, a lawyer. He bought me dinner at a nice restaurant. I worried about the price of the meal. When he got the check he said I was a cheap date. I wanted to ask if he'd pay my rent.

He told me he used to write articles on history in the early days of the internet. Corresponded with Victor Davis Hanson. He said he was broke into his fifties and then made his money in law. Married with children and grandchildren. He questioned if he should've stopped writing.

His life seems better than mine, but there he was, nursing regret over what he didn't do. We're stalked by acts never accomplished, loves never known. The past swells and subsides in its own rhythm. We forget who we were, but who we were doesn't forget us.

Summer passes by, July nears its end. A string of bright hot days broken by grey skies. Fits of rain. The summer of my life. Almost August, the crown of adulthood. Seasons return, the big show plays again. Histories, peoples, civilizations in cycles. Everything comes back except the only life you know.

Working at a café during the day and a restaurant at night, like last summer. The white noise of crickets on warm nights. There's more to do than ever and less of me to do it.

SUMMER OF LABOR

DRANK TOO MUCH AT WORK LAST NIGHT. Shots of tequila with the servers. Ducking away from the floor to chug pisswater in the prep kitchen. The night drags on and I'm surrounded by people spending five hundred dollars on cocktails and wine. Low lights and loud music. Walking around with jagged edges, raw nerves, heavy heart like a bag of bowling balls. Getting drunk almost makes me feel like I want to be there.

On a diet. It's called not having money. The poor man's diet. Indigent fasting. Coffee and cigarettes, acrid innards. My insides coated with industrial sludge. Organs like dying seals in spilled oil. A holocaust in my psyche but I look alright on the outside. Still going to the gym without air conditioning and deadlifting at a caloric deficit, head blanking out, pulling four hundred and seventy-five pounds off the ground.

I turn thirty-six in nine days. Asked my ailing mom for money to pay rent. A perversion of the natural order. She had me to take care of her but she's still taking care of me. You can do whatever you want, they said. I became a burden.

Hungover on a hot morning. Atmosphere of unwashed armpits. A smoke detector in the apartment building beeping for a week.

Someone new moved in across the hall. They have dogs. The last person had a dog that barked nonstop when she wasn't there. The new person's dog barks when I walk into the building. Knocked on the door to introduce myself. Heard a woman's voice yelling at her dog. She didn't answer.

The last three people who've moved in have been traveling nurses with barking dogs. The only other tenants are an old couple. Hans Moleman and his wife wearing plastic face shields and masks and gloves, walking with canes. The only time I see them they're running packs of bottled water from their car to the apartment. They live in a nightmare plague world, stockpiling plastic and eating Betty Crocker scalloped potato powder.

Fourth of July. One holiday after the next. Festivals and gatherings bind us, but in this atomized social environment every holiday feels like a haymaker to the jaw. Just when I've shaken off the concussion from the last one here comes another. Drive an hour and a half down the highway, always under construction, one lane for thirty miles, speed limit forty-five miles per hour. When I hit the brakes my steering wheel trembles. One tire losing air all the time.

Ninety-five degrees, my dad sweating over the smoking grill. Sun like a branding iron on my head. Hot dogs, hamburgers injected with cheese and bacon. My dad still bakes persimmon pudding for me every summer around my birthday. When you're a kid your identity fuses with a dessert. Your parents associate you with a cake until they die.

Gathered for a holiday, but we don't talk tradition, we talk television. Our memories are someone else's stories. No great deeds of people we know, no local lore, just fuzzy recollection of cartoon figures drawn by deviants. The only local news is my dad telling me he read about another kid I went to high school with who died a couple of weeks ago.

When someone dies in their thirties I assume it was an overdose. No wars to cull the young men right now, they do themselves in. The death of nearly everyone is a newspaper clipping glanced at by the elderly between tv shows.

SPOILED SLICE OF LIFE

SCROLLING THROUGH INDEED.COM until my brain bleeds. A bottomless pit of fake jobs, honeypots, phishing schemes. Postmodern business consultant performance art. Shell companies looking for conmen. Oiled up salesmen selling sales courses about selling sales courses by the seashore. Psychological studies, data mining programs. Scientists tracking correlations between job searches and the purchase of alcohol, firearms, rope, life insurance policies.

Thanks to my indeed.com activity, the Croatian mafia has my credit card number. Joke's on them, I have no money. Transnational corporations have my DNA and they're building an even more retarded version of me they can pay even less.

Apart from the scams, it's a thousand jobs fit for hunchbacks. Bell tower attendant. Cardboard box technician, pallet jockey. Warehouse picker/packers. Peter Packer picked a pair of picker packer jobs to pay the rent on his one-bedroom outhouse in an abandoned railyard.

Entry level, rear-entry level, subhuman level. The economy added four billion jobs last month, recently released felons and escaped lab experiments welcome to apply. Family Dollar is always hiring, paying wages that couldn't support a family in Burundi.

Or you need twenty years of experience shining penny loafers for the chance to write emails at Pindick & Skuddington. More important than ever to win friends and influence people. In other words: lie, cheat and steal. Exploit design flaws in the human psyche so you can pump and dump your way to a precarious six figure income.

The whole world is now a pickup artist bootcamp. A seduction quagmire. People are numbers, your past is a mass grave of instrumental interactions. A ladder of human bones. Everyone is looking for someone who isn't you. Including yourself. No one wants to work, no one wants to pay for work. So what do people want? Roasted turkeys flying into their mouths. A handjob from a hologram.

Society runs on menial labor no one wants to do or pay for or think about. Averting our eyes from all the scabrous delivery drivers and dwarves with pickaxes. Immigrants from the moons of Jupiter dropping off Tempur-Pedic sex chairs in the lobbies of luxury apartment complexes.

Progressives demand generous stipends to jerk off and comment on racist tropes in movies. Conservatives throw a fit when they're forced to pay someone for a task they'd otherwise have to do themselves or personally whip a slave to perform.

Fantasy used to be a supplement to reality, now it's the other way around. The simulation is your job, your lot; becoming a medieval peasant is the getaway.

I work doubles a few days a week. In the evenings at the restaurant until eleven, sometimes later. Next morning wake up before the dawn's ass cracks. Drive down potholed roads on tires with low air pressure. Get to the café, work five or six hours straight, no break. Run to the bathroom to squirt out some piss as quickly as possible so my coworkers don't hate me.

Empty stomach, dizzy. Can't order food, can't eat anything or people look at you like you're an orc. Everyone is there to stuff their fat faces with sweetened sausage but if you nibble on a turnover you're violating the health code, you're making people uncomfortable. How dare the people who serve you food also eat.

James Salter said life is meals. Maybe for that award-winning asshole. For me it's serving other people's meals.

Somehow I'm the only person who works in the service industry who feels physical hunger. Everyone else is on adderall, ativan, angel dust. These jobs are impossible without hardcore stimulants. Every industry depends on the pharmaceutical industry. Attention and happiness are prescription based. Good luck on your own. I'm using obsolete substances. Trying to keep up with the modern economy using coffee and cigarettes is like fighting a squadron of drones with a Wright brothers airplane.

My neighborhood is lined with maples and magnolias and three-story mansions. Esplanades of lush grass and fountains and sculptures. Next to my apartment building is a towering crackhouse. My neighbors wear ankle monitor bracelets and ask me if I can lend them five dollars for gas.

Behind the crackhouse is a shed where a stray cat hides her three kittens. I named her Gladys. She's a sweet girl, she lets me pet her belly. My girlfriend and I are trying to take care of the kittens, stop them from getting eaten by hawks and mutant squirrels. There are two torties. I might take one, her name is Eunice.

If I adopt a third cat, I cross the threshold from eccentric to circus freak. But I don't have much else going on. Maybe I'll qualify for government assistance.

NEW YORK MINUTE

FLYING TO NEW YORK CITY TODAY. I'm forgetting something. Underwear, driver's license, charging cord, power tools. Toothbrush and soap. Debit card, credit card, cash, money orders. Cyanide pills in case of capture. Some QR code that allows me to use the urinals. Need the right apps, passwords, accounts for all the services, access to trains, buses, little carts that sell turkey legs.

Haven't been to the city in years, don't know what it's like anymore. The crime, the trash, the atmosphere. People with long covid and other imaginary diseases wandering in a fog, anxious, deranged. I live in the Midwest. Not sure about the East Coast urbanites, the Democratic political machine, vax addicts, hypochondriacs, control freaks.

Travel planning can go to hell. I have to find a cat sitter. A ride to the airport. Bring enough clothes and toiletries to avoid smelling like a street person. I can barely find a clean pair of socks in my own home.

Murphy said everything that can go wrong will go wrong. What a bastard he must've been. The plane will crash, my apartment will burn down. I'll board a flight to Kuala Lumpur. I'll be robbed, pistol-whipped. Fall down a manhole. Eat a rotten kebab. Catch monkeypox, a new strain of covid. Arrested by secret police, thrown in a cell, nuts hooked up to a car battery. Diarrhea on the subway at rush hour. At the reading I'll drink too much, piss my pants, puke, have a seizure, say the n-word, sieg heil.

Everything has to work perfectly every step of the way. All the engineering and competence needed to launch people into the sky. The complexity of high-speed travel. The discipline and coordination of untold strangers. Mechanics and pilots showing up and doing their jobs, putting their problems aside. Blocking out divorces, foreclosures, dying parents, gay kids. Silencing the screaming world to focus on the task in front of them.

Everything I do, from eating sandwiches to watching movies to driving down the street to flushing bodily fluids, depends on a thousand strangers not getting drunk and fucking off. My everyday sense of independence rests on millions of tired sad people not sleeping through their alarms or jumping off a bridge. Some guy texting his virtual girlfriend at the wrong time will get me killed. One botched math problem and they'll be searching for my body among flaming debris.

Roads, airways, waste disposal, food safety. Regulations, committees and departments growing out of each other, responding to new technologies and disasters, new ways for people to scam and kill each other. Everyone checking everyone else's work, guaranteeing the one guy tightened the lug nut and flipped the on switch.

Division of labor, narrowing roles and increasing efficiency: at the same time multiplication of moments where everything can go wrong. One guy slips on a banana peel or looks at porn for a fraction of a second too long and planes crash into each other and a child chokes on a marble and a fruit stand falls apart and watermelons roll into the street and stop an ambulance from getting to the hospital.

Midday on the border of Brooklyn and Queens. I ate a weed gummy. I don't know why they call it getting high; it feels like I'm wearing one of those lead vests that protect you from an x-ray. Walking for miles on upheaved concrete, weaving around people, signs, fire hydrants. Stagnant heat and blinding sun. Grey t-shirt, pits soaked with sweat. Far enough from the skyscrapers, the congestion of Manhattan. Still, so many people and parked cars. More stores in a few city blocks than the population of my hometown.

Walking with my writer friends, those I've known online,

met in person yesterday for the first time. Good people, smart, generous, kind. But part of each of us is somewhere else, floating through digital networks. The way we live now; wherever you go, you're not there.

The night before it was the cityscape from the roof of Manny's apartment. The sky long and flat like a printed sheet. Soft reds falling into the glowing range of high-rises. We sat on the roof and drank beer and smoked cigarettes. The moon, shaped like the arms of an anchor, filled with blood and sank below the horizon. I was tired, smoking to stay awake.

A line of apartments, a long brick wall beaming in the sun. A blur of human types, jagged figures, cutout letters from ransom notes. Narrow streets, stores on every corner. Rows of trees swaying in the wind, their shadows like the tide.

Thursday afternoon before the reading and I'm nervous. I'll commit some gaffe, bore everyone to death, waste my time. Meanwhile it was announced that my novel *The Neighbor* made the shortlist for the Indiana Authors Award.

We get to the apartment where the reading is hosted. We bring enough liquor to kill everyone in Brooklyn. I chug beers and take shots. Talk to some people, meet more internet friends. I'm scheduled to go second but I switch with a poet and go first. I step outside to smoke a cigarette and a wild burly man, possibly Slovenian (found out later he's Greek and Venezuelan) hands me a joint.

Before I know it I'm on the rooftop with a microphone. Orange-tinted storm clouds, flashes of lightning in the sky behind me. I read. People laugh at the jokes. No slips, no tics, no flashbacks to the time in sixth grade when I played the piano in front of the whole school and forgot the piece and banged on the keys like a cat and went back to my seat and cried.

Afterwards we go to a bar. Someone brings coke. We stuff ourselves into the bathroom and I snort several bumps. A rush of grandiosity. I can do anything, feel like I have a hundred hype men within pumping me up. A band plays, the dance floor is full. Can't cut through the crowd to do more coke. Stuck among strangers, shaking, the music in my molecules.

We go to a disco and dance on a floor with those square tiles that change colors. Beer after beer, shot after shot, bump after bump, dancing and sweating and I don't know how I'm not dying of dehydration, cardiac arrest.

Not surprised people get hooked. Never done it before but within half an hour of the first snort I'm thinking *we need to do more coke right now. I need it in my nose. Crack open my skull and dump a bag of it on my brain.*

The night passes. I never come all the way down. We go to a diner and I order a burger and fries. I don't remember eating at a reasonable human rate. I'm pretty sure I ate the plate. Manny and I make it back to his apartment. I sleep for two hours, wake up with a slight headache and dry sinuses. It's time to fly home.

The whole trip has gone well. It can't end without a manslaughter charge.

LaGuardia airport. Packed in the plane, two seat rows. About to take off. We sit on the tarmac for three hours. The drone of the plane, revving up the engine and then powering it down, the crinkling voice of the pilot on the intercom. *Uhh, the only update is no update, we're still waiting to take off.* Flight attendant telling us we're not ready to go yet but they'll be passing out snacks and drinks. No cocktails.

Fuck your Sunchips, I need to be in the air right now or I'm going to slap someone to death. They cancelled the flight. Told us to talk to a gate agent. Had to stay another night and get a flight out of Newark the next day.

Murphy's law, except not quite. If everything went wrong, life would be easier, you'd know what to expect, how to feel. But life is more ambiguous, more difficult to resolve.

Back at home. Back to real life, my real identity as a man who wears an apron for work. No one at either of my jobs cares about my trip. My fantasy camp weekend. Why should they? I don't care about their stupid bullshit either.

A wild week followed by domesticated time. Like it never happened, slivers of a dream. New drugs and new friends, rooftop stage, a backdrop of thunder and lightning. A film of someone else's life. All that's left is putting cheese danishes in brown paper bags. Waking up before work with a feeling like I'm a death row inmate about to march down the green mile.

MY FAVORITE TIME OF YEAR

LATE SEPTEMBER DAYS, fading like all the rest. I wake up with my cat's ass in my face. Cold desolate apartment like a ramshackle barn. Joints popping on the walk from the bed to the kitchen. Resurrected not by God but a perverted necromancer. Animated by an alien will.

My water pitcher has an outdated filter, the sensor flashing red to remind me I'm drinking lead paint, mold, radioactive estrogen. I choose to believe that even a bad filter helps. I might drink a little less diarrhea concentrate. My bones feel a thousand years old. My brain born yesterday.

Fight the tide of dust. Tags from thrift store clothes, plastic lids. To-go coffee cups having found their final resting place on my end table. The momentum of waste, the grinding terminator implacability of trash and trivia. The essential drains to nothing, the inessential piles up to the barren heavens. Relationships, occupations, goals: less than scattered sand. Jeans with holes in the crotch, paper bags: more monumental than the pyramids.

Season turning, heat leaving the earth. Former coworkers invite me to a bonfire. They're not the worst people. I wouldn't celebrate if they were beaten with aluminum baseball bats.

Evening falls. Out of the city and onto the interstate. In my car with the crack in the windshield and the rusted catalytic converter and the flattening tires. If I hit one more pothole the glass will shatter and the tires will pop and the muffler and back bumper will fall off. Soon it'll be a Flintstones car.

Exit the interstate, the ground and sky level out as if pressed by a giant rolling pin. Corn fields parted by straight county roads. Indiana overgrown with a cash crop that makes people fat. Even the vegan diners with locally sourced rutabagas use our corn syrup and soybean oil. Suck on that, coastal elites.

Dusk gathers on the land. The moon like a rusted sickle. The road narrows, I turn into a private drive. Someone's uncle's house, a doctor. I arrive at what looks like a cult compound. Ready to be escorted by hooded acolytes into a torch lined grove.

Haven't eaten all day so I go for the hot dogs. Roast weenies and s'mores and drink some girl's vodka lemonade and smoke cigarettes. Think about how little I have to say to these people. Boyfriends or friends of friends I haven't met, no point meeting them now. I'm all out of meeting people fuel. I pet a Shiba wearing a sweater and then leave without telling anyone.

Last week I got a haircut at one of those barbershops with exposed brick where everyone has tattoos and high water Levi's and Chucks and Malcom X glasses and tight fade haircuts. When the barber finished he wheeled me around in front of the mirror so I could check to see if he'd cut any holes in my head.

I looked like I just came back down off Hamburger Hill. Never known any violence but I carry myself like I've watched childhood buddies get blown apart by car bombs. Never punched anyone and never been punched. I started a war within myself. No objectives, no way to withdraw.

Life eats itself, tears itself apart. Nature is a slaughterhouse, history a snuff film. I grew up in the safest place and time of all places and times. Comfortable middle-class upbringing in the middle of the most powerful nation in the world. Insulated and inoculated and educated and monitored. Still some dumb vengeful spirit slipped through to rake my organs. My inner landscape is cratered. My thoughts are agent orange.

Some would say I need more hardship, an external enemy. The cure for sadness is tormenting someone else. If you're not afraid or angry you're bored. Love fits in there somewhere, harboring hate in its bosom. Every advocate of love is one disappointment away from a Stalinesque purge.

October rolls along with cold dark mornings. The smell of woodsmoke and overripe fruit. Afternoons break into perfect weather. Sky so blue it hurts. Hurry and enjoy the fall before winter rapes us with an icepick. Pumpkins and apples and hayrides and flannel, gold and orange leaves on winding paths in the cool woods. Labradoodles and caramel corn and pies and cinnamon powder on your cider and pictures of every drink, every meal. Smile with a gun to your head, enjoy yourself before it's too late.

Mortal danger shows up like pop music, world historical events on and off the screen like one-hit wonders. I'm as plugged in as anyone and I have no idea what's happening. Not even enough to dismiss it sarcastically. What I do know is that my gym is raising its rates and I'm late on rent again.

The cost of everything is going up except my labor. Nothing gets cheaper except old electronics and people.

I might have an office job. Got it the only way you get anything, by knowing someone. Office management for an industrial construction company. Scheduling, emailing, organizing other people's work. They should see my bedroom.

I could become a white-collar stiff. The kind of guy I've served coffee to for ten years. Put on some loose slacks and groan about Mondays.

I'd make a little more money. Salaried income, benefits and paid time off. I'd sit on my ass, pot belly and anterior pelvic tilt like a Dr. Suess character. Eat takeout hot wings at 11:30 am. Work through the weekdays, take breaks to post comments on my cousin's Facebook.

There won't be women. It would be me and a few fifty-year-old white men and a bunch of Hispanics painting airplane parts in a hangar. I'd be responsible for other people. Talk on the phone to other fat middle-managers about slats. Get yelled at for fudging someone's paycheck, forgetting a meeting, ordering the wrong ink cartridges. Become a punching bag in a polo shirt.

But then I'd have to be that asshole that watches other people, tells them they've done something wrong; they need to hurry up. I've never overseen anyone's performance or led a team. I've silently judged everyone but let them shit their pants in peace.

All these jobs, the interviews, the screening; they need you to lie. Unless you're the kind of person who uses color-coded sticky notes, who has a whiteboard in their home. Yes, I'm extremely interested in maintaining order, I say. My toilet hasn't worked for eight months and I still haven't told the landlord. I brush my teeth in the kitchen because my bathroom sink won't drain. *I have to be organized, it's a must for success,* I say to a man who'd retch if he looked under the seats of my car.

They had me take a series of personality tests. The company pays for them. Learning about yourself always involves giving money to a charlatan. I answered the questions so incoherently I broke the test and had to retake it. There's only one question in a real personality test and it's do you think a personality test is an affront to the human spirit? The answer is yes.

When I said I wanted the job I was thinking about the stable hours and the money. Then I regretted it. They said they were considering other applicants and I felt relief. They scheduled me for a review this morning, a second interview. I have to leave in twenty minutes and I'm hoping an earthquake swallows my apartment. I hope the skies crack open and the four horsemen gallop through my neighborhood. Anything to avoid sitting in a starkly lit room in a squeaky rolling chair and pretending to be normal for an hour, pretending to want normal things.

No bigger lie than someone telling you they want honesty. I don't even want to be honest with myself. My soul is still in Brooklyn, lounging in a coffee shop during the day and doing coke at a disco club at night. I'd like money without needing to pretend to be interested in dull horseshit.

God save me from what I want. I'm a postmodern hedonist playing language games. An ageing childless millennial with two cats and a history of wrecked relationships, a culture war stick figure. My development isn't arrested, it's been executed.

If I had kids then I'd be more inclined to take the office job with *opportunities for growth*. Put in overtime hunched over spreadsheets, docking Manuel's pay because he was fifteen minutes late. If I were a married man with a rich social life then I'd happily work Monday through Friday for a family-owned small business.

But my social life is a wasteland with no wife and children on the horizon. If I stop buying abstract art sandwiches and books I'll never read, then I can pay the rent and afford cat food with my current job. More responsibility would be good for me but I don't want it.

I wasn't raised on hardship and duty, sacrifice or belief in something greater. Instead it was comfort and choice, doing what makes me happy. A life condemned to open-ended choice has turned me into a fatalist who can't choose the good.

Early morning opening the café, standing outside before the bustle, mauve light rising over the trees. Minutes later the sky shades pastel blue with red lines like a child's first drawing. Closed the night before, had to come in early to finish the closing tasks. Last night two women came in and sat at a table for an hour. Five minutes before close one of the women leaned over and erupted with neon orange barf. Like a scene from *Scanners.*

I put on gloves and a mask, used a roll of paper towels to wipe up most of the chunks. Mopped twice. Scrubbed and picked the extra particles of upchuck out of the cracks in the exposed brick wall. Held back my own vomit.

Leaning towards the office job, the career path instead of middle-aged meandering through the service economy. More responsibility but fewer piss splattered toilet seats, less partially digested pasta in vodka sauce and bile. So I hope.

One day off a week, a Saturday. The day when everyone in my charming idyllic neighborhood fires up their leaf blowers and dicks around with home improvement. Slicing sheet metal and redoing the siding while listening to classic rock. Letting their dogs out of the house. Relentless resonant barking, castrated beasts kept in apartments twenty-three hours a day released to scream and shit outside my bedroom window.

Kids out too. People love to grumble about how kids don't go outside anymore. They're all on the couch watching gay muppets. But every kid in my neighborhood is on a tricycle with a plastic gun, shouting about imaginary cataclysms, epic battles.

The quietest street in the sleepiest city in America bustles with the noise of a thousand steel mills, brims with the life and death struggles of a sweltering jungle; snapping alligators and giant rodents crashing through the brush. Rumbling trucks and arguing idiots. Towering gothic crackhouse next door written into reality by Edgar Allan Poekowski. Poor people yelling with the lung capacity of strongmen bursting hot water bottles. Rap Snacks and RC Cola giving them the strength to beat each other.

No one fights with Shakespearean ardor and eloquence like poor addicts. On one side I hear malt liquor bottles breaking and rolling indictments. On the other a dog barking whose shampoo costs more than what I make in a day. To my right a dilapidated drug den, to my left a Sear's catalogue nuclear family.

The life of a renter, the understudy of a street person. Squeezed between homeowners and hobos. Above me they're pondering what color they'll paint their spare bedroom; beneath me they're asking for spare change.

The noise of the modern world would have Schopenhauer roundhousing old ladies. The sensitive souls of the past whose delicate thoughts were obliterated by a squeaking fart three cottages down would tear their hair out and fling themselves into a river if they had to live in a quiet neighborhood today. How can a man think, explore the haunted warehouse of his memories with all the buzzing and clanking, car horns and shouts and bad music.

No peace anywhere for anyone. Now we crave the clamor. Earholes clogged with custom soundtracks, theme music everywhere we go. Pumping up or soothing ourselves into a drooling reverie. Listening to music to block out the music in all public places. Every person swaddled in sound. Field of awareness shaved down to a navel. You could walk up to anyone in public today and swing a 2x4 at their head and they wouldn't see or hear it coming. Rob people in front of their faces. They'd have to look up videos for an idea of who or what assaulted them.

GETTING AHEAD

AT THE SHOP WHERE I WORK six days a week and then I work extra shifts because one person gets food poisoning and shits liquid and no one else can cover the time because everyone else is working six or seven days a week or attending classes or studying for exams, this week I picked up a shift even though I needed to prepare for a podcast about E.M. Cioran.

I'd forgotten to pay the internet bill. The internet company that sends me forty thousand emails every day about new deals, more options, bigger packages, faster service and sternly worded warnings about service interruptions didn't have anyone on hand to turn my wifi back on after I'd paid the late fee and delinquent charge.

I had to ask the podcast guys if they could push the show back half an hour so I could go into my shop after it closed and use the internet. Tell the closer he needed to get out and that I'd finish his tasks after talking for three and a half hours about a dead Romanian recluse who wrote most of his works in French.

I hadn't eaten all day and I drank scotch and beer to loosen up. Forgot what I was talking about and the point I was trying to make in the middle of my sentences. Disembodied gaze watching myself blather. The hosts wanted to do another segment but my laptop ran out of power and I was so tired I was hallucinating, felt like I was talking to *Alice in Wonderland* characters. I think it turned out alright.

At the shop early before a Sunday shift. Haven't seen the sun in a week, maybe longer. Sun in retirement, cashed in its cosmic pension. Off to some resort galaxy, a condo on the beach, leaving us in the Midwest to shamble across dark frozen fields, our skin chapped and raw. Slipping on icy steps, hollow bones cracking.

Sky and earth merged into a gray miasma. The ambience of buzzing machines before the clamor of commerce.

Eating a vegan banana chocolate chip loaf. Lighter fluid after taste. Cruelty-free calories, the flavor of household disinfectants; licking the inside of a test-tube. All our pastries are vegan and gluten-free, made of the same material as those dinosaur-shaped sponges that grow when you add water. Vegan syrup, battleship lubricant. No animals harmed in the making of our products, plenty of animals harmed in the eating of them.

Rather than exclude a minority from any experience or activity, lower the quality so that all can pretend to enjoy an imitation. Never tell anyone *we don't have that* or *no you can't participate*. Deny people the pleasure of denial.

We look for pain and exclusion, the bitter thrill of rejection. When we try to satisfy everyone, we invent new modes of disappointment. Go underground for angst. Will to power is only half the drive. Equally vibrant is the will to impotence, the ingenuity of failure, the thirst for destitution.

The utilitarians and utopians discount man's love of subjection, humiliation, suffering and resentment. Our lust for the dictator, our fascination with cruelty. Not only our sadism but our masochism. Pity those who never experience the pleasure of feeling betrayed, the rush of bile carrying them beyond their good sense.

The man who misses out adds something to the world, bears sweetened fruit from poisoned seeds. The man who wants for nothing sinks into a bottomless pit. What he needs more of is less of everything.

End of the laundry cycle. Wearing tattered underwear, oil rag over my loins, ripped jeans, dirty shirt. White shoes stained with coffee grounds and syrup. Every task insurmountable. Need twenty-four hours to do my laundry. Put gas in the car, that's a day's worth of work. A half-eaten rotisserie chicken from Thanksgiving in my fridge. Scared to open the door, expect *Raiders of the Lost Ark* face-melting reaction.

I need yellow caution tape around my kitchen. Litterbox running over with turds. My cats shit like they're getting paid time and a half. Piles of paper grocery bags, empty boxes, cooking tools I never use. Most of what we buy is a tax on our fantasies. All those objects are placeholders for identities never adopted.

A folding leg card table in my kitchen. Haven't sat there once. My double, my unreal other, sits at that table and eats hot cereal, reads the paper and looks out the window. He's from another time, a time of analog mornings, local news, tin can coffee. Objects store our other selves; they hold the dead weight of possibilities.

(The purpose of all that furniture, those microwaves and toaster ovens, is to fill space, to see for us. The toaster oven with dust on its racks watches the corner of the ceiling for me, keeps it from caving in. All objects have their own point of view; together they patch the holes in reality. Without them our gaze would be sucked into an abyss.)

Another early morning, alone in a shop that will soon swarm with customers, guests, family members. I've been doing this for a long time. Haunting commercial spaces, brooding in godforsaken markets.

This is supposed to be normal. Same things day and night until you die. Enjoy your bread, dig your grave. We're pull string toys with only so much length. But the modern individual has been charged with a mandate from hell: innovate, create, chop up your days like a gourmet salad. Live a hundred different lives in one.

Used to be God or destiny that gave you a place. No shame in a low rank if that's where you're meant to be. Now we pitch other reasons for being less than we'd like: racism, the patriarchy, class conflict, communists, jews, etc.

None of it lands. Obsession with a man-made obstacle betrays a fatal truth: we're alone without reason to guide us. God's not around to take the blame anymore. We still have guilt, but no source, no center, no absolution. Which is why, rather than looking forward to an afterlife, we search for heaven while we live.

NEVER DRIVING HOME

ON CHRISTMAS EVE I CRASHED MY CAR. Lost control turning onto my street and hit a stone sculpture. Tore off the front right fender and smashed the can that holds the windshield wiper fluid. I drove the car back to my apartment and watched it bleed blue on the street.

Bald deflating tires on the ice. Last night the temperature dropped to negative eight degrees with a negative forty degree wind chill. Hateful, punishing cold. Instant frozen nose hairs, radical penis retraction weather.

Shouldn't have been out driving in that car. Symbols of looming doom on the dash. But I had to work out. Get under the barbell in a warehouse where everyone foam rolls, stretches, warms up with rubber bands and records their rippling buttcheeks. Where they pound out a thousand powerlifting and bodybuilding sets. Heavy single rep squats and five hundred tricep kickbacks. Texting and direct messaging between every set, posting stories on instagram, playing with the filters, repositioning the tripod, programming the arc of the camera-carrying drone, adjusting stage lights.

The average lifter spends twelve to sixteen hours in the gym. I'm in and out before they've finished warming up. I don't know how they hold down jobs and relationships. How they keep their pets alive.

Fitness as an identity, a devouring occupation. Niche elitist pastime. Health and strength as branding, self-promotion, an automatic answer to the question *what should I do with my time*. Increasing disparity through specialization of interests. The average person on the street looks like a bag of marshmallows. The average person in my gym exercises like an action movie star.

Many people eat fried plastic cheese dipped in thousand island dressing. A few freaks prep their meals; dose and time their calories like a model before a shoot.

The growing gaps in health, fitness, ability, education, wealth, beauty, charm. Many people appear blind to their own appearance. Others see nothing else. Society of the sweatpants. People in coffee shops and grocery stores looking like convalescents at a Swiss sanatorium. On the other end: women under thirty with smooth balloon lips, tight warped faces, acid trip lizards.

We share conditioned reflexes, broad behavior patterns. We differ in obsessions, products and services. Living the same way with less in common.

I had to get out on Christmas Eve. The last two days inside while deadly winds whipped the earth. Inside the poorly heated apartment, listening to croaking wood. Reading and napping and watching television. Prestige television. Miniseries, high production value, world class entertainment. Great film actors, professors of literature writing the scripts. Time-release television, one episode a week for two months. Never taken as intended. Instead it's eight episodes in one day. Watch so much tv you enter a time warp. Eight hours of electronic time become two hours of organic time.

Three seasons of a series in one month. Seven years of crime thrillers since I've last seen my family. I can't go on. Tell people I'm watching *True Detective* and they batter me with recommendations. *You have to watch this and this and this.* Leave my house after two episodes of high-end drama like I'm crawling out of a bunker after the end of the world. Blinking in the leftover light of a dead sun.

Thinking more about fictional characters than my character. Analyzing plot devices instead of calling my mom or volunteering at a soup kitchen. Not a brother or a son, not a boyfriend or a husband or a citizen, but a conduit of electricity, a socket. A set of eyeballs hooked up to a shallow pool of feeling.

My family postponed our Christmas gathering because of the weather. Haven't heard when we're getting together.

Might not happen. Waiting on the call, half-relieved I might not have to drive an hour and a half south in my busted car, pull up in the drive and watch my dad grimace, ask what the hell happened. He helped me buy that car, said it should last a long time if I took care of it. If I took care of it. He should know me better.

I don't want to bring this home, more bad news, more expenses. *How's work and what are you watching these days.* Eyeing the time for a respectful moment to leave.

Who is responsible for restrengthening family ties? Is anyone waiting for me to reach out or am I waiting for them? Unlivable tension of the individual in a narcissistic culture. Subject to overwhelming forces of disintegration, engulfing ennui, and yet also responsible, as if the decline is my fault and I could change everything if only I made the right moves.

My shop is closed so I'm drinking coffee elsewhere. New Year's Day, nine in the morning. I'm the only customer. Everyone else is asleep, head in a toilet bowl, hurling, dead. I fell asleep last night at nine.

Time for an inventory. Broke and bald. Average height. Good shoulder to waist ratio. Sociable for ten minutes, then I want to scurry off to a dank basement or a bell tower. Numb except for the odd spurt of despair and regret. Collapsing car, shabby apartment. Cats provide comfort and entertainment; they wreck my furniture.

Wife, children, respected position in the community: not even close. My retirement plan is to die of total organ failure in the middle of a shift.

Latte salesman for over ten years now. Experienced with mops, rags and steam wands. Reading job descriptions on indeed gives me a headache. Other people's jobs are a foreign country.

Too much of an attention span to watch youtube clips and tiktok videos all day, not enough of an attention span to read books like a serious person. Not retarded enough to succeed in the new economy, too retarded to learn.

Protestant middle-class background with no work ethic. Not even a consumption ethic. Not committed to hard work and sacrifice or decadence and leisure. Every quality interferes with every other quality. Uptight and lackadaisical and grim and frivolous.

Not old enough to feel the way I do, worn out, beyond it all. People pass through me like phantoms. I watch my life roll on like an aimless art school film directed by a bored ninny.

More hair in my ears than on the top of my head. I can stay in the gym for half an hour. Strength has peaked. Deadlifting and squatting and benching the same weight for months. Going to do steroids, go for that weird middle aged man tan, smoked meat skin, thick vascular neck.

A future of funerals. A past of ransacked tombs. Up ahead I see nursing homes and hospital visits. Anxious monitoring of vital signs. Screenings, spreadsheeting protein in my pee, cancer readings. No photo albums of children but a collage of my x-rayed organs.

Ageing alone, eccentric museum curator of old jobs, friends, girlfriends, apartments and appliances. *I once lived here, worked here, dated her.* No one around now was there at the time; every new person takes a tour through the ruins.

A Calvinist belief in predestination without God. Every step determined but no reason behind it. God is dead is not the same as there is no God. There was a God but he's gone. God is dead but so are we. Not possible to live without belief. What we have now is believing we don't believe. Idolatry of absence.

We killed God and replaced him with science and reason, then we replaced science and reason with therapy and politics. Personalized entertainment shaped by machines. The devices know you'll like this program. No end to the series, a fall into bad infinity. Need our shows more than heroin. More than we need each other.

Neil Postman thought we were amusing ourselves to death in the eighties. Television turned reality into entertainment. We've gone farther. Not simply passive reception of the spectacle but undead interaction. Donating our organs to keep media outlets alive. When you die from entertainment, your spirit doesn't rest or transcend. It wanders the wasteland, feeding on the remains of the social body.

Time doesn't run from us, we run from time. Rhythms of the earth too slow. Time wants to hold us, rock us in its cradle. But we've opted for acceleration, weightlessness, rocketing through an endless space of burnt-out stars. The earth wants to shelter us in darkness but we've covered the land in searchlights. Offered up every crevice to satellite spectators. Slaves to recognition in a disembodied dialectic.

From the electronic frontier to the algorithmic cul-de-sac. Phones in our hands like blinkers on a horse.

Hosted a reading at my shop. Brooklyn and Jersey poets on tour. Basement, exposed brick, downtown by our two blocks of skyscrapers. I drank cheap beer and read a short story. Drunk on the mic between sets, introducing the others, can't remember what I said. Hope I didn't talk about how Hitler made a few good points. All the buildup, the promotion, making a flyer, preparing the story, practicing. A blur of words and now it's done. No more recent or farther back than any other event.

Hosted one of the guys at my place. Restless night, worried about my cats disrupting his sleep. They're not used to strange men. Worked the next day. Still tired days later, will use the event as an excuse for another month. *Sorry, that one really took it out of me.*

Days sink like a stone without causing a ripple. New year feels like the old. Progress and decline look the same. Spending the reserves of my personal capital. Living like a twenty four-year-old and feeling seventy. I'll admit, it's fun on occasion.

FREE PARKING IN HELL

I WENT TO MY CAR AFTER A SHIFT and saw a yellow envelope under the windshield wiper. A parking ticket. The second one in a week. Nowhere to park but the lot of a nearby grocery store. Two-hour parking limit, license plates checked by lumbering simpletons in fluorescent jackets.

I haven't paid the first one. The charge has doubled by now. Tripled, they've frozen my accounts, raided my apartment, repossessed my furniture, abducted my cats. *If you do not take immediate action, penalties will accrue.* I'll be arrested; my Nick Nolte mugshot in the papers.

The city will get its money. They'll get my money and my time. My heart and soul. To avoid paying I'd have to call a bureau, wait on the line, talk to four different people. Appeal the tickets, go to the library and check out a four thousand page book on parking law.

I own nothing except myself. Responsible for something worthless, a magnet for tasks and irritants. Relieved of the duty to care for land, a wife, house, children; still busting my balls. Dragging my sack to the store and office and gym and auto shop and library.

Every day a case, an argument, a process, a serrated saw blade in the ass. Maybe you can convince the system to let you off the hook. Persuade bureaucrats to delete your file, lower the fine. Or you could avoid it until they suspend your license, revoke your citizenship. The system punishes you for trying to provide for yourself until you go broke and mad. Then you're eligible for assistance.

At every step someone tries to block or misdirect you. Profit from your insecurity and greed and lust, exploit your longings. Hold out empty promises and lead you into a back-alley beating. Hounded by the bumbling incompetence of those beneath and the tireless chicanery of those above.

Working a job not enough of a burden. You have to get to your job, find a parking spot, grease the security guards and lot attendants. Work for the opportunity to work. Pay bills, clean your house, improve every aspect of your being and sleeplessly ward off every corrupting influence or you'll get fired and your wife will cheat on you and your sons will become your daughters and the skies will rain blood and burning piss.

Everything around your job is a job. You know the original philosophers were stinking hobos because they thought prime matter was water or air or fire. Prime matter is work, labor all the way down, an infinite series of grinding obligations.

The world is composed of jobs and phone calls and forms to be filled out. Collection letters and voice mails from robots. Passwords and security questions. A universe of waiting rooms. Accepted or denied requests. Fractal patterns of official documents. Committees of ham-headed functionaries reviewing your record.

Division of labor multiplies obnoxious intermediaries, liaisons and representatives. Zeno's paradox of infinite middlemen between middlemen; movement is impossible. People make their living by making my living harder to make. Division of labor is subtraction of organic bonds. Almost everyone I know I met through an economic or electronic exchange. No human contact without an application, a contract, a bill or an app. Professional and romantic relationships nuked with a message, a phone call. Cutting someone out takes less than a gesture. Whole networks pulverized and reformed every six months.

Sick from the revolving door life. In and out all day long, chapped by pointless penetration, blunt entries and exits. Can't remember most of the people I've known. Faces and bodies mixed in a mosaic of the damned. I'll see them all in hell.

Been living like an idiot the last few days. What am I saying? For as long as I can remember. But more specifically the last week or so. Passing the days like a baton in a relay-race to death. No life of the mind, no vigorous inquiry or impassioned search for truth. Syndicated fantasy scraps adrift in my head. Characters and situations out of order.

A faulty projector run by a man smoking meth and swallowing barbiturates. I'm the director and the screen and the distracted audience. Smelly theater staffed by teenage numbnuts. Aisles and seats littered with encrusted popcorn containers from years past.

I don't think, therefore I'm not. Thinking or not, no being. Most of the time not there. Heidegger's foundational description of man as *dasein*, as being there, flipped upside down: instead it's *nicht dasein*, being nowhere, not-being all over the place. Hovering here and there.

I'm more of a Cartesian cogito than a phenomenological subject embedded in a lifeworld with projects structured by care. More likely to be tricked by evil genies conjuring a fake reality than surrounded by ready-to-hand equipment. Doubting rather than carrying tradition forward.

Three winters in one. Winter before time. Crippling cold. On days when the sun shines it's only a show of warmth. My insides remain frozen. Meat unthawed, frosted marrow. I note the pastel pink sky in the morning without feeling it, as if I'll feel it later. I'll live when I'm dead. No wish for sudden riches or widespread recognition. Only the vain hope that one day a sunrise will fill me with a joy that brings me back to childhood.

Hard enough to do anything when the world throbs, when color leaps from the leaves and animals rush around and bugs swarm in the air. All the same tasks await in the eternal cold and grey. Want to get under the covers under a pile of purring cats. Wake up months later to green grass and singing birds. Hibernation breath and bed sores.

Even going to bed is a labor for the ages. Turn off all the lights, brush and floss, put on pajamas. Seven hours later and I have to brush my teeth again, shower, feed the cats, shovel their turds. Shave my face, clip my nails. Buy new tubes of toothpaste, paper towels. Taking a shit is more work than I want to do.

Stayed up drinking and smoking joints last night and woke up late this morning. Now I can't meditate and massage my taint and gaze upon the dew and stretch my calves while the birds sing and the first light hatches at the base of the sky.

Check my chore list: only thing on there is everything. Before noon I need to clean the house and apply to jobs and call my mom, call my friends, finish my essay tutor profile and edit the short story collection. Each day opens with a three-hour window where I can move about the world without feeling like I've been hit with a tranquilizer dart. Today I woke up with the window nearly closed.

Even a slight hangover ruins all hope of action. Wake up feeling like I wrestled a gorilla. Missing gray matter. Blown out neural net letting ideas slip through.

My boss said I could help him at his warehouse today. Move boxes and take out the trash. He's not going to text me. I'd have to text him and even though I need the money I don't want to do any more work on top of the poorly paid work and unpaid work stacked to the sky, the minimal maintenance of life for a solitary man; sweeping the dusty floor of my apartment and going to the gym, picking up clothes and doing the laundry, cooking and doing the dishes.

Half the work is convincing other people to let you work for them. Nipping at ankles and trying to ride the hairs on a rich man's sack. Calling and texting and reminding *and hey just thought I'd see if maybe you still need someone to wash your cars and walk your dogs and teach English to your adopted African children and write your emails. Maybe I could do your taxes and ghostwrite an erotic letter to your wife.*

You spend the greater part of life convincing people to give you the chance to sit at a desk or stand behind a counter or stand on the sidewalk and twirl a sign or dance on a pole for them. All roles and occupations shift and pass away. Marginal opportunities arising and sinking and people flitting in and out like a slideshow. Swirling changes with stasis at the center. Stiff steps through a phantasmagoria, erratic wind whistling through your skeleton.

Spring bubbling up and flushing out the holdout winter elements. Color coming back to the land. Gleaming white magnolias and pink petals, wildflowers sprouting on lawns and esplanades. Most of the trees still leafless; rows of treetops like whiskers of a burnt broom.

Took a breath and my weekend is over. My leisure time is automated; some replica rests for me. My work is still manual, burdensome. No robots or slaves on the way for all the things I don't want to do. They'll simulate and automate all pleasure and joy and artistic expression, all triumph and drama, love and friendship and beatitude, the deepest human experiences, but work will remain real, necessary, physically and mentally taxing.

We've created a pill that will give you a prolonged orgasm and the mind of Isaac Newton. You'll fathom the logic of God at the creation of the universe.

What an advance. Do I still have to work?

Yes.

Division of labor boosts professional specialization. But on the other side, the breaking apart of extended family networks and the deterioration of sex roles drives personal generalization. An isolated person shoulders roles and responsibilities that would've been distributed by sex and place in a larger family structure.

(Within the division of labor, a narrowing of skills and interests occurs, a decline in practical and mechanical know-how. People obtain status and wealth not through mastery of material, but through mastery of others. Charisma, charm, the adoption of currently sanctioned speech patterns, a kind of empty adaptability, become critical factors of success. What emerges is the professional nobody, the amorphous manager, stripped of organic traits and beliefs, who manipulates impressions and gathers natural resources and gains renown through control of attention and behavior.

In the personal domain, this professional emptying is complemented by a fetishizing of interest and identity. Particularized compulsions, hangups, resentments.)

Even with appliances and devices and the technical outsourcing of family to machines, a single man is also his own wife and maid, his own father and grandfather and son. A laborer and a housekeeper and cook, activities manager and social director. He's responsible for seeking out his own wisdom and recreation.

The atomized self tends toward androgyny, in that it must carry out the work of both sexes. Desexualized workplaces, homes and organizations reduce differences to discreet organs. But these organs also become interchangeable, amenable to technological intervention. Only the biological being has a sex that is fixed by time and place, by organic composition, subordinate to a cycle; the technological being has inputs and outputs, links, parts with plastic uses.

Digitalization strengthens the disembodied forms of life initiated by industrialization. The body is sexually distinguished by its socially calibrated labors. Machines begin the process of translating sexually differentiated work into desexualized functioning, and a digital existence increases sexual confusion and disintegration by concentrating the self into a set of reactions to visual and auditory stimuli, a signifying chain circulating in a void.

The *cogito* of Descartes evolves from the thought experiment of a solitary genius to social reality, with people disconnected from their bodies and surroundings, prey to paranoid delusions, (in)secure in their self-relating doubt.

❧

Middle finger on my right hand twitches from time to time.

Could be Parkinson's or ALS. Or I might be dehydrated. Might happen for no reason. The odd quivering of the body, its malignant pregnancies, its noises and discolorations. A great surface of boils and rashes and warts, a canvas of ugly art painted by a petulant numskull. Even apparent beauty is achieved through struggle, punishing exercise and diet restrictions, stultifying routines. No matter how much effort you put into its preservation, the body declines, the skin dries out and droops, the meat spoils and revolts.

Nothing new under the sun except fresh aches in the flesh, new tears in the tissue. As time passes, the search for novelty gives way to the apprehension of oncoming maladies. Pleasure repeats but pain invents. No surprise that the body would generate the spirit as an attempt to escape itself.

There has to be something other than this hothouse of sickness. Consciousness is desire for separation from the body. All animals run from death; only man runs from its source, which is life.

We care more about the dead than the living. And we don't like living as much as we want to believe. Fear of death masks our fascination with it.

Last night I lay in bed with my black cat Marj. Parts of me were stumbling down darkened halls, old passages. For all the time I've spent with her, I know her better in my thoughts, my memories, in pictures and conversations where I tell others about her. She's more real to me at a distance. I know her better as an image, a word, a little story. But she will die before

I do, and when she does I'll regret not having known her better as she lived, not having appreciated her presence.

The impossibility of having a whole self: a part of you is never there, yet that absent part can't be expelled, forgotten. The presence of absence fractures the present. You can't get rid of what isn't there. The self isn't divided in the sense of comprising two distinct halves. Rather the self is split open. A line of nothing obliquely cuts through it. In this empty space a self-image forms, and it works as a guide, a reference for action. It also perverts and undermines our instincts.

Consciousness is an undertaker. Its concepts are coffins. People say we don't understand death. It's the only thing we understand. Life bores us like math homework. The most effective way to matter is to die. They say funerals are for the living, but life is for the dead.

The problems of life are insoluble, inscrutable. In death everything clears up. Everyone knows what should've been done, who someone was, what they meant.

Art, writing: death before we die, our corpse ventriloquizing our spirit. To write is to leave early, to steal significance from death.

Friday morning; a day from two years ago or two years in the future. Tomorrow is two days from now's yesterday. Mourn the end of what hasn't begun.

Lingering in the mood of last night. Second floor studio apartment, windows cracked. Air sweet and crisp like the skin of an apple. Power cables stretched against the sky. Moon blotched and bright. Viewed with old eyes, dimmed by millennia of myths. Worn-down wonder of every other civilization.

This morning already feels like the afternoon. Burns like a stovetop. Seize the day and remember that you will die. Carpe diem and memento mori. Once I seize the day, what do I do with it? Strangle it, feel it wiggle away. The very attempt to live in the present shatters its imagined purity. Seize these nuts.

Hollywood writers are on strike. I'd like to strike some writers. They can trade places with me. Not for a whole lifetime, but for one year. Maybe two. I could pump out a few dozen movies about Batman's sexual identity disorder (*Batperson*), remakes of *Groundhog's Day*, *Fast and Furious 37* (*Slow and Senile*). Hollywood writers can work in my café and make pineapple syrup for our signature latte two or three times a week. Buy a pineapple and coconut cream and cut the pineapple and mix the cream and sugar and water and strain it four times. Answer questions about cortados. They can clean poop stains off two toilets, sweep and mop the floors. Listen to people in meetings and interviews. Watch first date fidgets and expired couples ignoring each other. Pictures taken for instagram; cups of foamy milk that will soon be shooting down urethras.

The phrase *living paycheck to paycheck*. Not even that. A chasm between the checks, a broken bridge over crocodile infested waters. They can try that out while I lean back in a swivel chair and come up with quips for digitally rendered heroes in armored underwear.

LETTERS TO THE EVER UNBORN

SMOKE FROM CANADIAN WILDFIRES drifts down to the Midwest. An otherworldly pall hangs over the land. Air like a smeared screen. A notification on my phone about staying inside but I ignore it and walk around. My throat hurts, my eyes water. There's a deathly calm, a stillness in the trees. The birds sound hollow, like museum reproductions of extinct species.

Flames engulfing great northern forests. Natural and

unnatural disasters. Woods turning to flesh-melting mist. Rolling odor of things that should not be burned. That smell from childhood when you put an action figure in the microwave.

You hear about distribution centers blazing, trains running off the tracks, planes plunging into the ocean. God's wrath, but man isn't happy with himself either.

We've engineered a system that degrades nature and mocks the divine and we hate ourselves for it. Accidents and errors as self-punishment. We deserve the worst but when it comes it's never bad enough. We can't make ourselves feel as good or bad as we'd like. For that we need help from on high.

Where is that Old Testament asshole, the jealous vengeful god with the fireballs and floods. He's still here, lost in a crowd of idols. It's a problem of scale. In the old days he judged and punished fewer people. He has to work harder for recognition now. Causing earthquakes and tidal waves and brutal conflicts and plagues and bizarre animal behavior but he's competing with streaming platforms and media personalities for attention. Our personal projects muffle his thunderous warnings.

Everyone pronounces their own truth. Not Ten Ccommandments but one hundred million strongly-worded suggestions. Advice from all angles. Scientific sounding explanations from apes with credentials. Instead of a single stone tablet, a billion etch-a-sketches. Twiddled-in moral codes.

❧

Aliens, financial crashes, wars, riots; leper colonies in the richest cities, dispossessions, foreclosures, people fleeing political unrest and private demons. Shootings and stabbings, clips of men spilling blood and caramel macchiatos on sidewalks outside starbucks. Virtual carnage superimposed onto tranquil mornings, floating photographs; copper-tinged sunlight like scattered pennies, the soft sheen on brick facades. Squirrels chasing each other on dry green lawns and up the trees, the sound of their nails scratching the bark.

Warm pre-summer nights on the steps of my apartment building. The velvet darkness decorated with streetlights glowing white like pearls. The murmur of a fountain down the street. Evening solitude. On the love seat in a cool apartment lit by lamps. I want to double the quiet lonely hours, let them settle into me. Also, I want it to be over.

All that time worrying and I find I worried for nothing.

Every emergency forgotten, shoved off stage by another crisis. Bored of yesterday's catastrophe. Standardized panic, algorithmic alarms. Machines fueled by mishaps. Fake events and real events look the same; real people sound like tv characters and tv characters sound like realistic cliches.

Desensitization is adaptation. We must fit within a norm, no matter how ugly, dysfunctional and odd. After a week, the latest innovation feels like what we've always done. The body brings in foreign materials. Burning silicone in the air: we say a few smart things and then ignore it.

The world ends not with a bang, not even a whimper, but with annoyingly articulate commentary. Informed idiots bouncing their steel-plated heads against each other in the comment section. Not a bang or a whimper but a new tv series and a new girlfriend.

If trumpets announced the apocalypse, they'd stop

screaming and we'd go back to work. The world never ends and that's why we can't stop dreaming about it.

❧

Knausgaard's autumn. Meditations on apples, frogs, the sun, lightning, tin cans and beds. The stuff of everyday, the scattered shapes of nature. Interspersed with letters to his unborn daughter, his fourth child. The man has been married three times and now has five children. He's said that he's made a Faustian bargain, that his success has come at the cost of his relationships.

At least he's successful. Worse deals are out there. You could trade relationships for professional and artistic failure. You could send ten women to therapy and in exchange you get a chicken salad sandwich.

I could also write letters to my unborn daughter, but she isn't forming anywhere. She's less than unborn. A gust of wind in the vale of my heart.

Letters to an ultrasound image of my nutsack. Apologize to the tadpoles in my testicles. I'm sorry I squandered you. Treated my sacred tool like a squirt gun at a pool party. My little wrigglers: I'm sorry I launched you everywhere but where you're supposed to go. You want to live but you're misused by someone with mixed feelings about life, gnawing doubts about its goodness.

Maybe it's you and not me. You might be happy swimming in circles and then crusting up on synthetic fabrics. I might be acting in accord with your wish to waste yourselves. I don't know if I'm overriding my body's drive to reproduce or if I'm faithfully carrying out its highest aim.

Half of my unborn daughter shoots out of me every day. The other half bleeds out of women in Indianapolis, Chicago, in New York City, Washington DC, in remote German villages. I'm a jewel beetle leering at the curves of a beer bottle. Only the emission is accomplished.

My unborn daughter; I'm not saving you from the environment, capitalism or the patriarchy. I'm not holding back from having you because of underfunded daycares or a defective education system. I'm saving you from myself. You'd thank me if you could.

THE SMOKEY CITY

I NEED A BREAK. A long one. So long there's nothing to reattach myself to. Need breaks around the breaks, an extended intermission. Let's all go to the kitchen and grab ourselves a snack and slip into a coma for five hundred years.

Not a trip or a vacation. No festivals or fairs or concerts, no crowds or lines, no wafting stink clouds of armpits and fried food. Don't schedule a day at an amusement park or water park. No planning and deposits and credit card information.

No reservations and verifications and finding someone to take my shifts and feed my cats. Spare me the hassle of buying tickets and receiving confirmation texts, downloading apps that connect me to Burmese boatmen. Signing up for services and newsletters and updates on deals. Sleeping on a friend's floor or in a hotel bed or an Air B & B. Shitting in strange toilets.

Give me a break that doesn't include telling people I'll be in a certain place at a certain time. That doesn't require me to check out the local bookstore/coffee shop/cocktail bar.

Give me the opposite of the late Anthony Bourdain's life. No dinner on the beach under a thatched hut. The lulling rhythm of the waves, the breeze on my skin, savoring the crab sauce as a taffy-colored man with crooked teeth wistfully recalls his youthful days zipping around on a motorbike and getting beaten by his father. It can all go to hell. I'll take the early Anthony Bourdain life; I'd rather work in a kitchen and do heroin.

I'd rather stare at my ceiling fan and think about Kant. Think about my dire economic condition, my health. Not sick now but I'm working on it. Hope I'll have the strength to throw myself out a window when my lungs bleed or my colon explodes.

I need free massages in my living room. Buttery handjobs from a woman whistling Debussy. Not a fun date at the new barbecue shack and shooting range. No one ask me to go hiking or paddle boating or llama riding, no tedious foreign films or readings or comedy nights or open mics.

Give me three months without texts and emails. Without updating everyone and hearing all their updates. *I'm tired are you tired what did you do last night what are you doing later what's new. Oh that sounds exciting that sounds promising that sounds exhausting that sounds stressful; you got engaged you got married you got divorced. You got a new puppy your cat has diarrhea you went to a restaurant and the vodka penne was rich the music was too loud the hostess was rude.*

How was your meeting, how many meetings do you have today. (These days we're a meety crew. Large-scale organizations teeming with teams. Zoom conference calls, screens with thirty smaller windows and blurred lumps in the center, alien children's magic marker approximations of people. Mishappen stacks like melons fallen off a truck. *Hollywood Squares Brady Bunch* opening sequence.)

The obscene intimacy of a digital meeting. Piped into a stranger's home where outlandish acts occurred ten minutes before the call. Submarine scope of a polyp's underwater pit. Looking up at flabby neckflesh, into hissing noseholes. The view of a fly under a swatter; placed like a plate of chicken strips before a panel of fattened jackals.

Have you watched this did you know the brother of the police chief was also in sons of women he played the guy in the band with the cokehead girlfriend no not that guy he was also the scumbag in kings of anarchy he was the guy who took that other guy out to the parking lot and smashed his skull with a tool box.

No more catching up on real lives or fictional characters. Leave me behind for the love of God.

Going to Chicago tomorrow for a reading. I won't be reading

but I'll be supporting e-friends. I did everything I'm reluctant to do. Bought bus tickets, found a place to stay. Still don't want to do anything. The bus will break down, blow a tire.

Heading north, closer to the toxic wildfires so I can breathe in the acrylic air. Satan crop-dusting North America. I'll come back with an extra arm, the abilities of an x-man. I'll have fun despite myself. Four days off from work: I don't deserve such luxury.

The Greyhound bus broke down. Old girl needed a rest. A little past Lafayette we rolled to the side of the road and died on a bridge. Scummy river below. I thought about getting out and plunging into the turd-tinted waters. Or walking away. Not toward home or Chicago but in some other direction, nowhere, a town with a boarded-up post office, one stoplight, cows roaming overgrown lawns.

We sat for half an hour, maybe forty-five minutes. The driver fixed the problem and we rumbled on our way.

I knew this would happen. Something would go wrong. Though it wasn't as dramatic as I imagined. There was no bomb, no deadly feud between Keanu Reeves and Dennis Hopper. Just your everyday ass pain when you try to do something nice for yourself, something nice for someone else.

On our one hundred and sixty-mile trip, we stopped four times. The bus was packed. Each time we stopped an assortment of nimrods shambled off and smoked. I wanted to say: fellas, we're wasting time, let's get to where we're going and then we can chug a carton of cigarettes.

I sat next to a man with a whistling nose. The woman in front of me smelled like a urinal cake left in the sun. At one stop I watched a man puke before getting on the bus. He was sick. And not like he'd eaten a bad clam.

Buses these days: sometimes I think about the violence and rage and loneliness of the car, and I think we should reform society, collectivize transportation; cut down on exhaust and accidents, roadside bludgeoning. Then I ride a bus and think about traveling in my own tank. I believe in the public good until I'm out in public.

I get why there are so many humvees and military grade vehicles on the road. People talk about the militarization of the police; what about the militarization of the public. Every person armed with machine guns and pistols and surveillance equipment and knives and pepper spray and lead pipes, enrolled in street fighting classes; townhouses and sedans outfitted with state-of-the-art security systems.

But then you have the apologists and enablers of criminals. Those who look away from mobs looting jewelry and liquor stores. An unpredictable public pumped full of contradictory messages, castrated and empowered, passive and explosive. The bewildering sense that you could get away with anything or nothing. You could scam and cheat and steal with impunity, harass and intimidate strangers, stomp a man's wingtips on the subway and no one will intervene. Or your amazon smart fridge could shut down when you send the wrong tweet.

The point of money isn't to afford nice things, it's to avoid the underclasses. Levitate above the hunchbacks and boiler room toilers, the scrapyard pilferers, the booze soaked and piss-logged and overdosed and undernourished. The desperate requesters, panhandlers and street performers.

What money buys is iron gates and stout guards, smooth transport between luxury apartments and high-rise hotels. Good schools, safe streets. All technology improves life in a specific sense: by protecting us from others, increasing the breathing space between us and the swelling ranks of unwashed asses. Every connection is a barrier. The point of every close relationship is to insulate us from everyone else.

We made it to Chicago and I had enough time to eat a sandwich and drink some coffee and smoke a cigarette. I walked as fast as I could to meet with Sabrina and then we took an uber to the venue for the reading. A record shop or video store with cassettes and 45's and who cares.

I drank beer and liquid THC and spaced out and then zoomed back in. Everyone did a great job. Too much literature. Too much art. There were films and musical performances as well. I can only hang so long. I had to wander the streets and smoke and drink beer elsewhere.

People bemoan the lack of good art, standout artists. *Where are the vital voices of our generation* and so on and so forth. They're everywhere. Working full-time jobs, raising children, running from their families, sleeping under awnings, draining their trust funds. They're rich and poor and well-read and illiterate. Every kind of art from every kind of person is available. Art isn't the problem. It's everything else. It's love and death and war and work and politics and the existence or nonexistence of God.

I don't have money to support all the good writers, all the working visionaries, all the great burnouts and wash-ups, the truck-driving and bartending and jack-hammering poets, the dry-walling playwrights and software engineering novelists. I can barely afford indoor plumbing. Barely have enough time to read the dead legends, much less the living.

Thank God for summer dusk. Warmth without humidity. Backyard of my apartment building, time alone, almost alone. Hanging with the neighborhood owl, soothed by his hoots. Lightning bugs glowing yellow-green like alien embers. Streetlamps like stage lights in a deserted theater. Swaying leaves casting shadows on graveled alleys.

July is a momentous month. I turn thirty-seven tomorrow. In two weeks my short story collection comes out. I'm hosting a reading at my shop. Thirty-seven years old. When my parents were my age they had two kids and owned a house. Today I'm using my birthday money to pay the rent on an apartment with a broken toilet.

A few days ago I met with a woman, a manager at a marketing firm. We talked about a copywriting job. She said she's looking for someone with experience. When she described what her firm does all I could hear was big band music. She said I needed to put together a portfolio. I'd sooner do gay porn.

I don't blame anyone else for my low station, my tumbling out of the middle class. Boomers, immigrants, lizard elites; it's not their fault. I'm allergic to opportunity. Single, bald and broke. Two books to my name, two cats in my keeping. I'm under no illusions: I'm screwed. The problem is I don't mind.

READING IS DANGEROUS

I TOOK TWO WEEKS OFF FROM WRITING. Two or three, I don't
keep track. I don't keep track of anything. It all gets crushed.
The last ten years like a flattened beer can.

I lose and forget, ignore and neglect. Bills, recurring charges,
renewals. Book sales and page views and subscriptions. My
driver's license expired on my birthday and I haven't renewed
it yet. I'm another Unregistered-American. Black market
firearms racked on the window, coke powder and weed flakes

on the dash, baggies in the backseat.

Chipmunk chunks in the glovebox. Mexican day laborers in the trunk. Phone full of missed calls from creditors, various 4th-party agencies, bounty hunters. Mailbox stuffed with letters from utility companies with bright red stamps on the envelope. *Urgent response required.*

Breaking the law isn't only a positive act. It's not only stealing snack cakes from the gas station or jamming a fire poker into someone's brain. You become illegal by existing, by failing to fill out the proper forms. It's not enough to eat and shit and sleep; you have to keep up with payments, update your status. Go to sleep for a couple days and wake up in a world that doesn't recognize you, that'll banish you to the outer reaches.

These days a man is more numbers and images than flesh and blood. A composite of representatives and accounts. Not an approximation of an archetype, but a manager, a public relations greaseball, an animal hiding its fear and despair behind mirrored gestures and echoed assurances. No more grand sacrifices at savage festivals, no hearts ripped from chests or heads rolling down the steps of a ziggurat. Instead it's daily concessions, an ongoing superstitious performance. You don't throw a virgin into a volcano to appease the sun, you display flags and repeat terms and tick boxes to please functionaries.

Writing lets me leave it alone. What a gift. Everything else, everything equivalent to sticking my dick in a hornet's nest: I have to do it every day, multiple times a day.

August came around fast. July was a gauntlet of events. Birthday and book release. Hosted a reading at my coffee shop. Had four readers lined up. Promoted it for weeks, had people put up digital flyers on instagram. The day before the reading two or three people called the shop asking why we were hosting fascists, right-wing writers. They sent messages to the owner; they said the space wasn't safe for the queer community.

The café where I work and sometimes hold readings is a gender-neutral, androgynous abstraction of a business, like almost every place now. It's designed to attract anyone with a caffeine and sugar addiction. Commerce doesn't care about your inborn identity, your family bonds, your traditional religious beliefs, your ties to the land, your moment in history. All enterprise wants is your mouth and your asshole, your drives. In the modern market there are no divisions of race and sex and religion, there are only compulsions.

We're queer and poc friendly, supportive of all types, skin colors, disabilities. We're so goddamned friendly you can hardly believe it. We're here to answer your questions and make you feel comfortable, safe, seen, heard, acknowledged, accepted. You can safely enjoy a cup of coffee, a latte, an espresso soda and a vegan coffee cake for a reasonable price. Sit at a table for eight hours and write emails, attend zoom meetings, organize your orgies.

Most places are like this now. Except maybe Curbstomp Café in Diddleville, Alabama. But someone thought the readers I picked for the reading would create an unsafe space because they've been published in Expat Press, which our anonymous concerned citizen called a far-right publication. Expat has published trans writers, gay writers, drug addicts, scenesters, everyday working folks, trust funders. People from all over with a range of views. Say whatever you want about the quality of the writing but unless you've got a bad bout of typhoid fever, I don't understand why you'd think it was a right-wing magazine.

An anonymous commie twitter account posted a tweet that named the other three readers. I have work published in Expat press too, but I wasn't mentioned, even though I hosted the event to celebrate the release of my short story collection. How many hate crimes does a man have to commit to earn a little publicity?

When I heard there was a problem, I wanted to cancel the event. The original deal was that one of the writers would be taken off the bill because he'd written some serious no-no words in a short story that some soviet cosplaying dipshit couldn't recognize as satire.

The reading was fine. I drank an indeterminate volume of beer. Everyone read their material and no one was beaten or harassed. I didn't sleep that night and went back to work the next morning. I was so exhausted I couldn't see straight. Customers looked like lava lamps.

Some time has passed. The reading is over, the book is out and I'm still working. One day at work feels like two days, one day off feels like an hour. What you love is barely there, what you hate hangs onto you like an orangutan.

More to say about people's inability to understand and appreciate art. But that's not my subject and I don't care enough to produce a balanced and mature essay about it. I'll leave it to those who don't create to argue over who should say what.

The sideview mirror on the driver's side of my car is broken. I don't know who did it or how it happened. Could've been anything. A tweaker headbutted it at four in the morning. A bird flew into it. A squirrel chucked a nut.

Fractured glass, mirror bent up. When I look to my left I see the sky and passing branches. Disorienting vision of a shattered world. Every left turn and lane change is a blind man's lurch into the unknown. I'll miss the gas truck barreling down on me, the immigrant child on a moped. Carnage coming my way; oblivious, whistling as I turn the wheel toward a fiery death.

Not instant incineration but medium heat sautéed skin. Caramelized tissue finally cooked down to the bone. Rookie cop retching in the heat. People passing by, going to work or to the store to buy water filters, toilet paper, baking trays, frozen meals. Emergencies and errands. The intermingling of banality and tragedy.

(Awareness raising efforts usually juxtapose your casual existence with someone else's hardship or gory death. They should emphasize the reverse. *In the time it takes you to vomit up your organs, 30,000 people finished their ring dings.* The person who drives past your life-ruining accident furrows their brow in the cereal aisle of the grocery store ten minutes later. How long after your death rattle do your loved ones turn on the tv. How long before grief is overtaken by the taste of a ground-breaking mayo flavor.)

The latest problem with my car. Rusted exhaust and catalytic converter and a flattened tire. Check engine light, maintenance required. Splash guard scraping the ground. A new clanking sound, a metallic popping on the right side. Signs of oncoming collapse. Something horrific could happen anytime, or not. This car could outlive me. The threat of disaster raising my blood pressure. Ignoring my own check engine lights, the symptoms of a stroke. I could have a heart attack on the road and my car will make it to work. A dead man delivered to the coffee shop; everyone still gets their lattes.

❧

Summer slides along. I retain little of the passing days. Memory is an empty idea, an atavism. *Remember when people used to remember things? Huh.*

Someday I'll search for lost time. Until then I'll be looking for a job, a clean toilet, a new life. I don't have the luxury of retiring to a cork-lined room and mocking the snobbery of my declining social class. Practical needs overshadow artistic aims. In search of an affordable sandwich. A morning without dread for the approaching day.

What I experience is neither smooth and dark enough to count as nothing, nor is it textured enough to register as an impression. The question isn't why is there something rather than nothing, but why can't we settle down in one or the other? All action somewhere between manual and automatic. Without control but no sense anyone else is in charge either. Gods and elites equally unreal; curse words for when I stub my toe or forget to pay a bill.

Sensations of the summer. I've had a few, now that I think of it. Look through my notes to help me remember that I lived. Mostly it's been smoke breaks on blazing afternoons. Sitting under the Japanese maple in the courtyard, red leaves like a blood-stained shuriken. Some skies thin and colorless. Others low and heavy. An unmoving atmosphere like I'm trapped in tupperware.

I'm properly alive for about three hours a day. Early mornings and four shots of espresso. A little writing, a little reading. Then an hour or two at night, on the shores of sleep, the pleasure of drifting off. The rest of the day is a yawn.

Summer felt good for a few seconds. Unseasonably cool temperatures. Now it's heat advisories. Air quality warnings. Deadly weather. Man and nature in a protracted murder-suicide. Good riddance to us both.

Got an application at the pipefitter's union. An apprenticeship program. Might be time to try manual labor again. Last time I worked for a carpenter. It was supposed to be a return to man's proper role, covered in sweat, erecting houses, hammering functional forms out of the wild tangles of nature. I was so bored I wanted to saw my head off. Plus the guy I worked for was a dick. But then so am I. At some point we would've attacked each other with power drills.

The service industry always takes you back. Like a desperate ex-girlfriend. Of course she's seen a few other men while you were gone, but she can still use you, and you know what to do.

Serving the public, the half or quarter of the population that fills its pointless days with meetings, consultations. Some wear shiny loafers and others seem outfitted for two day hikes in the Ozarks. Fifty pound backpacks, gallon water bottles, trail mix, grappling hooks. Sitting in shops for hours. A bizarre mix of rugged outdoor wear and advanced digital technology. Two laptops and at least one phone, surrounded by screens like they're issuing commands at NORAD. Airpods pumping custom soundtracks into their brains, dance music from outer space.

One last thing. A few evenings ago I was sitting on the back steps of my apartment. A barred owl flew down from a tree and landed in the yard. He stared at me with his abysmal black eyes. Turned his head and drank from a dirty puddle and looked at me again. Seemed to say *you didn't see anything.*

OUT OF PLACE

INDIANAPOLIS, THE CITY OF STOPLIGHTS. More construction cones than people. Where you see red fifty times a mile. Every other street blocked off, lanes closed. Weedy fields and gravel lots. A city of decaying factories and blooming luxury apartment complexes. No manufacturing of physical objects. But plenty of new buildings for the temporary housing of transplants.

The *smart* people here work in real estate and web

development, tech start-ups. Always on the phone, on the laptop, in the middle of a meeting. They work in coffee shops next to the nursing students, the future medical professionals. Sweatpants and scrubs. Spreadsheets and email accounts alongside diagrams of the lymphatic system.

Two kinds of public space now: the café where everyone works and studies and holds meetings about work, and the courtyard between the café and grocery store where two old men chug a fifth of vodka. Shaved heads gleaming under ceiling lights or the autumn sun. Two kinds of people: the remote worker and the drifter. Both uprooted. Both staring; one at a screen, the other into space. Both talking to some invisible person far away. One always on time, on track, coming and going. The other outside of time, living by unscheduled impulse.

Five pm on a Tuesday. Eighty-seven degrees in early October. Basement café of brick walls and glass windows. Like a kiln in here, the sun pounding the panes. Every table taken, no one talking. Vaporwave playing at a low volume. People might as well be in test tubes or cryogenic capsules. In a wax museum society, a tomb of neo-Egyptian aristocrats, buried with their electronic baubles.

The silence of the individual in public is achieved through an uninterrupted flow of private chatter, a near-constant though discontinuous production and consumption of data. Silence and stasis in physical space determined by digital activity. For a time the coffee shop was considered a third place, after the home and the office or work site. But if the public now wears pajamas and works in the shops then there's no essential difference between any of these places.

The shop feels like an office and a composite of living rooms, bedrooms and bathrooms. The primary product of the shop isn't coffee or baked goods but an electrical charge: all-day wifi. The secondary product of the shop is an illusion of public presence, of participation in a vibrant shared world. No word is more popular among transient strivers than community. To use the electronic infrastructure of a shop you need a password, generally a nonsensical jumble of letters and numbers. To use the dilapidated social infrastructure you also need senseless passwords like inclusion and community.

BREAKING UP WITH TIME

DAYS OF DISTRACTION, sluggish toil and uneasy leisure. Bright and cool mornings, tangles of power lines and tree branches, flattened clouds like foam on the waters. Moving in a circle and a straight line at the same time. Doing what I did yesterday, the week before, last year. Heading toward death, the one unrepeatable event. The only thing always out in front.

Time outruns everything, including itself. I started out with plenty of stamina, a good gallop, elastic hamstrings. The years slowed me down. I need more energy to move a shorter distance. The past outpaces me, too. Heraclitus said you can't step in the same river twice. You can't step in the same memory twice. We remake the distant past with materials close at hand. No real reunions.

Or we desert time. It could be our fault. After giving up on eternity, we averted our eyes from the moment. The eternal was supposed to redeem the inadequacies of the temporal. We pinned our love and hope on what passes and our constitution crumbled. Now we can't face the fading present. Digital technology attempts a resolution between the impossibility of the eternal and the insufficiency of the transient. Digital experience is neither ephemeral nor immutable, but a denial of both.

The digital milieu, with its scrolls, feeds, clips and pics, fuses the discontinuous with the continuous. Time is defined as discrete bits of information in a fluid medium. A seamless passage of representations without origin, end or inner relation to each other. Moments that, in the specific technologically structured way they pass, obscure their momentary character, blunting our sense of the impermanent in a wash of formally preserved impressions.

In Kant's transcendental philosophy, time is a form of intuition, one of the conditions of possible experience. All objects, including our apprehension of ourselves, appear to us and receive our categorizations through an internally structured flux. The electronic device reproduces and physically concretizes the virtual construction of internal time. In effect, today we primarily bear sense-making instruments in our hands rather than in our heads.

While human evolution has always involved an exchange between the brain and the tool, between what the hand can grasp and what the mind can think, today most of the thinking and calculating happens in the external device. Soon after Kant, the question emerged: what is the basis for the conditions of possible experience, if we don't accept that they fall onto our skulls like a cinderblock from God? The answers included history, tradition, a dialectical or dynamic spiritual process, class domination, and evolution as adaptation to changing environments.

All experience presupposes a formal structure: passive spatiotemporal intuition and active conceptual determination of objects. These forms were rooted in a variety of conditions that shared the quality of *having been passed down,* which is also the quality of *being able to be passed down,* whether in the genetic code or on the historical and cultural level of mnemotechnical transmission of thoughts, values, discoveries and impressions that make up a heritage, through which both individuals and collectives distinguish and preserve themselves.

The difference now is that the forms of intuition and understanding are no longer accretions of history and culture and evolution, but stimulated responses to mass-produced tech industry artifacts and subscription services programmed to maximize consumption and advertising revenue. A rapid deformation is occurring, or an obliteration of existential structures. Without a durable past informing present experience, the future is eclipsed, and people increasingly renounce the continuation of their own cultural and genetic lineage. Formal selection criteria by which a person interprets his experience are decultured, subjected to market manipulations and the influence of homogenized mass minds linked by a uniform adoption of digitalized habits.

The commonly decried compulsion of photographing and recording all events amounts to the industrialized externalization of experience, a disburdening of the pressure to maximize enjoyment of fleeting sensations and scenes. For there can be no internally consistent standard by which to measure a successful appreciation of the moment, and so experience is outsourced, distributed in networks and stored in databases. When participation in eternal life no longer compensates for inhibited earthly enjoyment, mutilated experience is translated into a technologically reproducible form, a facade of the infinite.

A single life needs the support of the historical and the timeless. A ground and a goal. We've tried every kind of replacement for religion: art, politics, history, technology, even other religions. Thrift store spirituality, bric-a-brac beliefs. They all fail, they result in death and despair. A few spasms in a void, toothless gnashing.

It's not man that needs religion, it's religion that needs man. And religion always gets its revenge, appearing as cheap copies, haunting and misleading us before finally sapping us of our absurd vitality. Man doesn't seek, he is sought. Which is why those who spend their whole lives in a state of curiosity never find anything.

Religion and social form are reciprocally determining. They flourish and decline together. The reduction of religion to a useful tool of organization marks the dissolution of social bonds.

(Unless you hold the esoteric idea that only the enlightened

few can live with the truth, that religion is a human creation in a chaotic universe. History is then an argument among arbitrarily gifted spiritual masters, a rhetorical and philosophical war over which ideas and values will rule otherwise amorphous masses.

The modern experiment, a scandal and a blunder from a traditional esoteric position, consists of democratizing dangerous truths formerly limited to elite thinkers, and gambling on the possibility that revealing the underlying chaos of reality will empower people in general to become creative arbiters of their own lives. This perspective greatly overrates the influence of thought on behavior and underrates the complex interaction of ideas, social instincts, technology, environment and history.

Going farther, it rashly and arrogantly characterizes religion as a force under human control to be wielded for utilitarian purposes. The reasoning moves backwards; religion is defined as a coarse attempt at answering questions about purpose and meaning, questions that can be answered or even dissolved by science and philosophy and engineering. But the questions come after the answers, they arise as retrospective rationalizations. Or we can say that religion unveils itself as a question-and-answer compound, a call and response without some preceding period of nonreligious or instrumental questioning.

One last note: in the modern democratic age, we tend to see writing as straightforwardly polemical and shamelessly confessional. The writer stridently identifies enemies and shamelessly exposes his inner workings and outward allegiances. Interpretation is then construed as an exercise in uncovering what the writer said without intending to say it, unmasking his hidden biases and the historical conditioning of his statements. The possibility that a writer might intentionally mask his message or communicate it obliquely, for instance in a parenthetical aside, or as an idea he seemingly dismisses, is mostly overlooked.)

A day off like the first breath of air after having a plastic bag around my head. Back step of my apartment building, ten in the morning. A cock crows two houses down. When did my yuppie neighbors get chickens. The cock keeps hooting. I'm awake you asshole.

If it's not a rooster it's a barking dog next door or in the backyard of the house behind my building. Power saws and leaf blowers. Children screaming and laughing and crying. Pickup trucks rambling down the alley, beds overflowing with junk, waterheads rifling through the dumpster. The modern world is a noise machine. My neighborhood is quieter than most of the city and it still sounds like a Looney Tunes cut-up of a fat man tripping over trash cans.

Just wear noise-cancelling headphones, you might suggest. Soundproof your apartment with mineral wood and vinyl. Stuff fiberglass insulation in your ears. Fill your shopping cart with sensory-deadening materials, prophylactics.

I need blue light blocking spectacles, noise-cancelling headphones, sunscreen, water filters, latex gloves, condoms and cyanide pills. Block buttons on all my social media platforms. I'm walking out of the house wearing a bicycle helmet and a bulletproof vest. Progress is counteracting the effects of previous progress.

Last week at the shop a vagrant stole a woman's bike. I was working and noticed a shabby man pacing outside. I couldn't go out there with a hammer because I would've been guilty of profiling, acting on sound instincts.

By the time I noticed he'd grabbed the bike he was pedaling down the people's trail. A brick path, flat and smooth, perfect for stolen cycling. I chased him. No traffic that day. Four intersections in a row wide open. I gave up and watched him glide away.

Back to work, a line to the door. People still need their lattes. Back to steaming milk with steam coming out of my ears. Why try to stop petty crime? Because theft offends something in me, some lingering sense of decency that somehow sits next to my urge to kick every customer in the groin. The man could've had a knife, a gun, HIV-tainted needles, venomous snakes and spiders and starved rodents in his pockets and still I went after him. I don't want you in my shop but I'll throw myself into danger to save your stupid bicycle.

Square in the center of autumn. Air like a damp cellar, hints of spoiled fruit. Aluminum grey skies and then a clearing. Incandescent oven light baking the cursed earth. Dead leaves littering the streets. A gust of wind now and then. I want these moments to last but that's because I know they won't. Time and I: we're destined to betray each other.

THANATOGRAM

SOME PEOPLE LOSE THEIR WHOLE FAMILIES in a firebombing. In terrorist attacks and bus crashes. Grisly home invasions. They lose limbs in factory accidents and woodshed mishaps. Drunk uncles with shaky grips on circular saws. Fingers gone in a flash. Blood spattered ceilings, an irreparable cut between before and after.

Some people lose functioning in their organs over a long period of time. One day their heart stops or their arteries burst like pressurized pipes. They don't see it coming, they downplay the signs. A little chest pain now and then, the occasional whiff of burnt toast. Then they wake up in hospitals, coffins or urns. Reclining on a cloud or roasted on a spit in hell.

I lose my keys. Once every two or three months. My body is magnetically charged to repel crucial objects. Those essential items that unlock doors and guarantee my identity. So far I haven't fallen in front of a running tractor or been pulverized by a nuclear blast, but I can't live for half a year without getting locked out of my house or misplacing a debit card or driver's license.

Fat days shuffle along and then they're sucked into deep space. Nothing happens except what tends to happen. Habits weave into other habits until they form a fabric so thick it suffocates. Changing my routine becomes one more routine, another mechanical task. Cultivating chaos with systems, enhancing creativity with procedures and methods. Nothing happens except the regularly scheduled outburst of the irregular.

It could certainly be worse. I'd rather get locked out of my house than have my head lopped off on camera. Rather tell strangers on the internet about the inconveniences that punctuate my life than appear in a widely circulating video of my undignified death. Shot in the face over a parking dispute, brained by a flying chair in a brawl at a Church's Chicken.

In my day-to-day life I work among people whose nerves nearly shatter over a tense word at the cash register. On the internet I watch videos of men emptying their pistols into fathers and sons in apartment hallways. Shootouts at the Golden Corral.

Death on the digital installment plan. Not simulated violence but real violence in the form of a simulation. Agonized flesh converted into bits and spit back up on the screen. From ashes to info, from dust to data. A formerly anonymous everyman's last twitch gone viral. Repeated a hundred million times with a hundred million comments.

They say parts of your brain register what's on the screen as real. At the same time: our brains determine what's real as a technological production. Centuries of anti-foundationalist thought, spreading secularization, the systematic undermining of transhistorical truth. God is dead and so are we but our machines live on, capturing and reproducing the ghostly reverberations.

I grew up in a safe place, long cleared of natives, scalpers and raiders. As well as wolves and giant cats and venomous snakes. A vast landscape free of man-eating plants and swamp creatures. Every aspect of my surroundings has been designed to protect me from danger. My upbringing freed me to engineer my own downfall. Which is less dramatic than drug addiction or a gambling problem. It's a simple inability to manage complexity. Staying on top of bills and keeping track of personal belongings. I've tried to avoid as much responsibility as possible and I still have to act as a middling bureaucrat of my own meager belongings, a social director of my dilapidated networks.

Sometimes I wish for enslavement to devices and megalomaniacal executives. Go ahead and implant chips in my brain, in my wrists. Get rid of objects I could lose. Brand a barcode on my neck that grants me access to feeding and sleeping pods. Construct a social system without the need for cars and homes and tools and yards. Drop me in a gerbil terrarium with tubes and wheels and pellet dispensers.

Weld an apple watch to my forearm and glue smart glasses to my head. Replace my body with an amazon exoskeleton. Increase my IQ so I can appreciate differential equations or decrease it so I can enjoy marvel movies and monster truck rallies.

The elite plan for the average global citizen is to own nothing and be happy. I'm pretty sure the actual outcome of that plan is almost everyone getting machine-gunned into mass graves, but in those moments when I'm searching the sidewalks outside my apartment for dropped keys or replacing flat tires of my rusted out corolla or trying to think of how to make more money, I can't help but look forward to a future where my possessions are reduced to a tunic and a wooden spoon for ladling gruel, where I'm shuttled to various viewing stations and given repetitive tasks that contribute to the social good. Not that different from the present, where autonomy is imaginary but the burdens are real.

Fall hangs on. We've been gifted with blue skies and warm weather. Patches of yellow and orange leaves on the ground shining like fresh vomit. The tree-lined streets of my neighborhood awash with radiant light and eccentric shadows. Right now I can't get into my apartment. I'm waiting for the maintenance guy to bring me a new key.

I had a week off from work. Not a paid vacation, not part of a benefits package. Even though I worked five or six days a week for over a year. In my industry you don't get paid time off. If you come down with an illness, drive your car into the Grand Canyon, need emergency surgery for head trauma, cardiac episodes, aneurysms, then you still have to find someone to cover your shift, you lose money, your cats starve and the electric company shuts off the power to your apartment. In my line of work the best-case scenario when you can't show up is that you piss off everyone else and you eat a bag of flour to save money.

I mistimed the transition from one job to the next. Still don't know when I start my next job but I was able to pick up a few shifts from the place I just quit. The time off refreshed me so that I could return to the public in a cheerful mood. When the first customer walked to the counter I wanted to blast him in the face with a fire extinguisher. True happiness eludes us on this foul planet but I feel much better about existing when I'm not at work. At least this kind of work.

Years and years of employment in the *service industry*. I don't care for the phrase. Sounds like I clock in at the blowjob factory. Spend ninety percent of my day on my knees chugging sack sweat. Same/different fuckers day in and out. A revolving door community of meat masks. People with flexible working arrangements. As opposed to working stiffs like me. If only my job had the same flexibility. Make a latte eight hours after someone orders it. Steam a cortado while I take a shit. Read Robert Burton's *Anatomy of Melancholy* before handing someone their croissant.

Thank God for the electric employees and their flexible

schedules, their loose stool timetables. The people who sit and scroll in the shop and go to hot yoga across the street. Sitting and stretching and bending and adjusting all day. Wielders of western technology and dabblers in eastern spirituality.

(The secular and uprooted digital coal miner indulges in a pastiche of vaguely traditional, mystical or therapeutic practices to cope with the dizziness of working and living nowhere, so long as those practices are filtered and commodified by token gurus and corporate functionaries and insofar as the surrounding decorative beliefs don't interfere with smooth economic exchanges.)

It was found that standard issue computing devices and the postures they impose are worse for the skeletal system than a lengthy stay in a Vietnamese bamboo bird cage. Now companies make adjustable platforms for laptops, so that people can sit up or lean back with their screens angled for minimum strain. A coffee shop full of people like astronauts about to launch.

History turns its pockets inside out. Progress is a prolapsed organ. Sometimes a name is the only thing linking an institution of one age to what it becomes in another.

Think about the nearly liquidated tie between the contemporary café and the coffeehouses of old. They used to call them penny universities because a few pennies for a cup of coffee bought you the experience of hearing pompous jackasses argue about religion and politics in person. Coffee and conversation and radical newspapers. That's what used to bring people into the cafes. Today, every coffee shop would close if it ran out of syrup and wifi.

Pumping and squirting flavor solutions where people set up

their flight simulators and send messages to outer space. Without signature lattes and personalized electronics the coffee shops would be overrun with rats.

Not that I want warm conversations with customers. But that's my fault. Some people look down on small talk, but it's perfectly fine in its own right. It's the frequency, rapidity and repetitiveness that vexes me.

You can talk about four or five things with slight variations. The weather is a legitimate topic because it concerns us all; it's a truly democratic subject and a solid basis for establishing comfort. Very accessible. It doesn't matter where you went to school, who your parents are, which epic historical figure you're pretending to be online. When it's cold everyone can feel it, *even though it's been a little warmer than usual for this time of year, but the nights have still been getting pretty cool. I think it even dipped below freezing last night, had to scrape the windshield of my car this morning, but today's supposed to be a high of sixty-five, you really can't ask for much more. Oh yeah, it was way colder last year around this time.*

Small talk is part of my job, and the best way to get me to hate doing something is to pay me for it.

I get paid to be convivial in churning transactional environments, and that makes me a little cranky. The old leftists used to call it emotional labor, which is now a term used by people who expect financial compensation for having family and friends. I'd prefer to keep love and money separate. Protect at least a few things from corruption.

During my week off I went to Brown County and spent the night in a cottage. I made friends with a calico cat and hiked through the wooded hills, my boots kicking up fallen leaves colored like faded bruises. The night sky was brilliant with stars. In the silence of the countryside I could hear the humming of the earth.

A place where human encounters are less frequent, where small talk fills out the expanse. But also a place I have to pay to visit, where I can't live because there's no work. Unless I get some typing gig and they deface the land and sky with cell towers.

Wind that feels like it came off an ice cap. A day so bright and clear everything appears made of crystal. I don't know if it's time that declines or if it's my soul that can't get up from the couch. Time might die without us urging it forward.

Each afternoon I dwell within a different body, a dummy with my likeness, but with the reason for living removed. All the hidden animal acts still occurring, my planted parts at work. What's missing is spiritual volition. The pulse of memory and expectation. These afternoons lie outside duration. They don't break down; they sit like stones.

Afternoons that blur the mornings and block out the evenings. Somehow we move beyond them. They too pass through us, though we hear them like a gong's endless echo.

Life engenders the desire for something other than life because so much of it is gummed up with dead time, dead selves. Stalled passages, shells and rinds we can't digest. The experiences we cherish happen on occasion. The rest of time hardly registers except in our shame for failing to retain it.

I live with two cats in a one-bedroom apartment. Where light through the blinds lets off a dull sheen like oxidized meat. An apartment that traps chilled air and leaks heat through the windows. Without wifi, less outfitted than a cosmopolitan camping trip.

In my living room the evening opens and I look toward sleep. Few things as pleasurable as the ebb of awareness. We fall asleep with the assurance of waking, and so enjoy the abandonment of our selves. It's only when eternal darkness looms that we dread closing our eyes. Unless we've had enough tired days, unless our waking selves have already left us.

Going to sleep is one of my favorite things to do. Not being asleep, but approaching it, or feeling it approach me. Mingling with shadows and phantoms. The unclenching of identity. Branching out like vines in a thousand alleys.

If falling asleep lasted any longer it would turn into a torment. If it happened any faster it would be nothing. An act or experience without substance that we can't separate from consciousness or unconsciousness. The closer we get to sleep, the farther we move from ourselves. Or, it works in the other direction. In sleep we coincide with ourselves, pure night, abyss, the dreams and nightmares of history.

(What is the dreaming self, and where does it take place? We might say inside our heads. But it's an interior that we experience as structured by a difference between a self and a world. Although this inside is more external than our waking consciousness, more volatile and phantasmatic, and the outside world of the dream is more intimate and imaginary than the

environment we move through when awake.

When we're awake, we distinguish between our internal experience and the world outside us. When we dream, this very difference is folded entirely within. Or is it?)

All things present as reversible. Everything rotates, flips upside down. The external world melts into fantasies and our desires take solid shape. Every conceptual scheme, every value system blends into its opposite. All objects exhibit mutually exclusive characteristics. Time is a chunk of cement or a wisp. Our life is entirely within our power or completely dependent on what outstrips our understanding.

I went home for Thanksgiving. Put in my time visiting family like another task. Those who gave me life and share my blood, we meet as awkward ambassadors of distant countries. Forgetful historians of a common past. I don't know how to repay my debts to them, uncertain as I am about the value of life. We all vaguely gesture toward the nature of time. We all get old, we say, and it's not clear if we're terrified or resigned. Or even hopeful.

We don't speak of God or death, truth or illusion. The television plays and we eat meatballs and persimmon cookies. The farther apart we drift, the less time it takes to catch up. We abridge the long passages.

My ninety-two-year-old grandmother didn't recognize me at first. Then she couldn't hear me. My mom couldn't hear either. Most of what we say is barely worth saying once, much less three or four times.

They have my odd book with stories about hookers and cannibal butchers and dollar store shootouts and patricidal madmen. Hard to say if they like it, if they know why I devoted all that time to articulating bizarre scenarios instead of finding a career and getting married and having kids.

The name I inherited, that stretches back into a past I'll never know, now sticks to stories about diarrhea and junk food, failed relationships and alienation and the persistence of miscommunication. I had all the opportunity anyone could ever need to be normal. Models of middle-class decency. Some like to say the social conditions have changed, and that's true enough. Still, I've made my choices, and I can't link my background to my present standing.

What I'd want my family to appreciate, what I'd want anyone to grasp, is that even a bleak story speaks to the joy of creation. Every negation affirms some power, however marginal or despairing. I need to remind myself from time to time.

THE NEW YEAR

THE COLD; IT DOESN'T COME FROM EARTH. Heat kills but cold *is* death. Space, emptiness. Total coverage, perfect immobility. Fire breaks down organic structure, turning solid matter into smoke and ash, but cold destroys through binding. Everything else dismembers in some way, threatens the unity of the body. Cold destroys by slowing down, keeping it all together. Highlighting the *threat of unity*.

Walking around my neighborhood, afternoon off. Even

when I'm not working I remember my days in shifts. The off-time relative to the on-time, the paid time. I could never work another minute and I'd still describe the days as off, days I didn't work.

My mold is set. Either free or employed, the free always filled with some other work. I treat rest like another field of tedium. The ideal of inaction forever out of reach. Hustling to figure out how to relax.

Three or four kinds of weather this winter, a young winter that doesn't know what it wants. The seasons don't know what they're supposed to be. Neither does anything else.

Time not as a fluid passage, but a shuffling of snapshots. In the long windows of great brick buildings, the setting sun gleams like melting steel. One evening among others, a trace of a trace, sparse notes without a primary source. Hours of dry air and shining light, then a different day, cold and wet like a sneeze. Grey skies of greasy wax paper.

My six-hour work week. Tim Ferris hobo lifestyle, passive negative income. Not an email job but an email hobby. An amateur on the internet, suboptimizing health and habits. I can last one more month on my savings and then I'll have to work at Long John Silver's.

Apply for a fake job on indeed and the bots flood my inbox. The counter for everything real resets to zero, the siege of copies never stops. Reality used to impose itself on you, while fantasy was your own doing. Now illusions flush your brain and reality is something you laboriously construct, rip from the earth and beat out of people. Programs want to know you; they're tracking your fluctuations, flaring on your screens, seeping into your digital cracks. Meanwhile everything else drifts and skitters around you like candy wrappers in the wind.

Easier to give everyone a show than a role. More episodes and films than anyone could ever watch, but not enough jobs, houses, relationships, places on stage. Cultural and technical systems clashing; not a good idea to bring everyone up on the idea of their own singular personality, their unique perspective, when work is mostly pressing buttons in anonymity.

History indicates a dynamic conflict between two senses of auto: the autonomous and the automatic. Sometimes the two terms are synonymous and sometimes they contradict each other. From one angle, we consider ourselves free when things happen automatically, without struggle and deliberation. We also define freedom as independent, consciously chosen and managed action, which places autonomy closer to the realm of the manual, the crafted, the local project.

Automation supports autonomy up to a point, and then it subverts. Imagine if you had to consciously control your organs, will your heart to pump blood. We relish the mechanization and automation of certain labors. But automation tends to accelerate, take on a mindless mind of its own, and subsume what was formerly singular, creative and spontaneous. The promise of ease inclines us to translate more of our selves into the automatic, until there's nothing left except a ravenous appetite.

Most people don't lament the loss of organic memorizing and calculating functions. They don't miss the manual labor of the mind, the grunt work of the soul. The less repetitive and tedious our work, the more time and energy for the unreckonable, so it seems. In practice, we can't cleanly separate automation and autonomy. No longer needing to calculate or remember becomes no longer being able to calculate or remember. The technical and memorial aspects of free, independent activity also degrade, and the outcome is submission of all conscious acts to programming, industrial scale production of art and culture.

Technical objects and minds always form circuits through which memories pass. The written word does some of the work of memory, but those records require conscious reactivation, a specialized and independent focus that also draws on automated mental operations. This conscious experience of externalized memories, also known as reading, opens channels for rewriting, creative interpretation. The handing down of a tradition that lives insofar as it changes while remaining recognizable.

Autonomy must be kept in tension with automation, without one subsuming the other. The inability or refusal to work and make manual decisions, to grasp and craft in a traditional context, will enslave us to mechanized appetites, turn our spirits into obsolete equipment.

❦

Still no snow, just winds with a chill from a sunless space. For us the year begins in the frigid depths. Call it a new year to forget that we age. A trick of the calendar. Ageing without advancing or recollecting, a little like freezing to death.

❦

The last two nights below zero. Single digit temps during the day. I thought it was cold before but like everyone I didn't think of how bad it could be. Would be. Decline isn't hypothetical. It could get worse but then it's also guaranteed. I rarely admit the goodness of the moment because I'm dreaming about how much better I could feel, how much improvement the world needs.

To appreciate my current present (my now now) I need to imagine how it would feel to cut off my feet with a circular saw. I think I'm cold but I still have feeling in my fingers. I could be stranded in the mountains, buried under snow. Hands and feet stumps of black ice. Anus frozen over. I could be four days without food, half-mad with fear but aware to the end.

As of now I only feel discomfort, a distraction. Nothing like the force of an indifferent, destructive nature or a murderous divinity. Civilization holds so much inherited wealth that even a dipshit like me can survive deadly weather. I don't know how to stream hot air into my apartment but I can flip switches and adjust dials. I work a *job* but I don't need to know how to do anything else or even why it matters if things work or not. Specialized division of labor has me working to be almost useless. I hardly know what to think about it.

My world consists of services. Not primarily of things, of material or even people. Today I mostly experience people in the mode of service. Not face to face, but face to interface.

I know a little about how to negotiate and exchange but nothing of duties. The world came before me in the armature of accomplishment and I don't know how to adopt it and carry it on. I see our machines and our morals as nature, I assume these man made systems will keep working the same way the sun rises and sets. Responsibility for society sounds as strange as feeding firewood to the sun.

(Except we used to burn wood for the sake of the sun. And much grislier things. The traditional act of sacrifice; ritual killing in consecration of life and a power beyond. Today you only read about it if you remember it at all. In the old days we felt responsible for the gods. Now we're not responsible for a chicken sandwich.)

In Ortega y Gasset's *The Revolt of the Masses*, the mass man is defined not by economic or social class, but by his bovine complacency. He takes civilization for granted. For him, the machines and services and systems run like inexhaustible rivers. Mass man demands nothing of himself and everything of the world.

Ortega y Gasset uses the term mass not in the sense of size, but in the sense of inertia. A mass doesn't move of its own will, it must be pushed and shocked. Mass man reacts to his circumstances and asserts ownership of opinions and abilities that have been fed to him.

Modern technology doesn't so much eliminate work as it conceals the spirit behind the work. Automation creates a false impression of stability by obscuring the concentrated effort that goes into designing, building and maintaining complex systems. The digital mass man is fractured, atomized, reactive to stimuli and ignorant of the techniques supporting his body and the principles informing his mind.

Ortega y Gasset called him the self-satisfied man, but nowadays, things are a little more complicated. The masses don't assume institutions will automatically endure. Instead, they believe they should tear institutions down. Civilization will collapse; we should not only let it happen, we should encourage it, speed it along.

To the extent that mass man today is capable of action, it's in service to destruction, inversion; preserving by perverting. But even this tendency is programmed, institutionalized and commodified. Today we gain power by claiming to resist it.

(The despair and resignation in the face of an approaching cataclysm. People say they don't want kids because the world will end soon. The end of the world is decried, but then the refusal to procreate ends the world even faster. Society is stocked with people who'd rather break the board than play a game they don't think they can win. Denial of the tragic nature of life on one side, denial of redemption on the other.)

It's tempting to say of various things that they're in retreat, withdrawing, disappearing. More accurately, the decline of any phenomenon, any practice or idea, happens by circulation, saturation. For instance, sacrifice; the notion is frequently invoked, but almost entirely in profane contexts that water down its meaning, its specificity. Sacrifice is synonymous with earthly economic exchange. You give up something to obtain something else. Whenever anyone wants to talk tough, from whatever angle, they bring up the need for sacrifice.

What is sacrificed is no longer sacred, as there's no bond between the human and the divine. Therefore no propitiation, no responsibility and no gratitude. No bond between the human and the divine also means no bond among humanity.

Market relations for us all the way down.

Who or what plays the sacrificial role today? Everything and nothing. Ritual violence gives way to random violence. From the terrifying show of power to the impotent outburst. From the staged spectacle of execution to the accidental explosion caught on camera. Violence, like sacrifice, has no place; as a result, it's everywhere, if only as potential; lightning about to strike, or static electricity that makes our hair stand up. Sympathetic nervous systems on alert.

Traditional sacrifice spills blood to affirm the indestructible creative power of the lifeforce, the animating spirit underlying all things. Blood also expiates the guilt of the living. In death, the sacrificed spirit returns to its source and returns the community to its origin.

For us, death isn't a passage back or beyond, but a technical error to be fixed or a welcome end to a pointless struggle. Life extension and life denial go hand in hand. Bio-hacking and assisted suicide: the two poles of our profane administration.

My car won't start. Turn the key in the ignition and the dash lights up and then nothing. A dead battery or a bad starter. Maybe I ran out of gas. Could be a busted undergirdle.

I don't know. I'm hardly a man. Primary and secondary sex characteristics but no *tertiary* sex characteristics: things like know-how, mechanical skill, interest in the stock market.

Protecting is a little different: I'll hurl myself into danger to protect loved ones. It's about all I can do for them. Use my body as a shield. I can absorb bullets and knives and fists; all other services call for a tradesman.

In school I ignored the hard sciences. Hell of an unsubtle classification. Hard science for hard men. Where a flubbed number brings down bridges and starts electrical fires.

I leaned toward the soft sciences, the humanities. Only soft women are supposed to care about humanity. Music and literature, the accoutrements of a high-class whore. When something goes wrong with a tool I read a book on what went wrong with the modern age.

But this time I tried and cleaned the corrosion from the car battery. I went to AutoZone. Haunted relic of a business, setting for a Stephen King story. People who work in an AutoZone you never see anywhere else. You wonder about their lives for five seconds and then you forget about them.

I bought some battery cleaning spray and a wire brush and gloves. Sprayed the battery and scrubbed the caps and dried them. The car still wouldn't start.

Perfect timing because I don't need to go anywhere. I don't have a job. Meaning I have no money to fix my car. I need a job to pay for my car so I can get to my job. A loop like a noose around my neck. I need things to pay for so I have a reason to keep working. My only responsibility is putting a roof over my cat's head.

Otherwise why not drop into the bowels of society? Float in the sewage among those stripped of everything but themselves. Eat dampened fried chicken out of styrofoam containers. Suck cigarette butts from garbage cans. Stumble into coffee shops with blood rimmed eyes and crusted spittle on my lips.

Getting around in a city built for cars. I could ride the bus but I'd rather run with a pack of wolves. No bike. I sold it for sandwich money two summers ago. Relegated to my legs (back to the bipedal) in time for bleak winter. An expanding blank space.

Walking under skim milk skies, intermittent rain. Old man winter's swollen prostate piss drizzle. The same bleary color from earth to heaven. Winter, the season of the unseasoned, the indifferent. Sleep and death and ungiving ground.

Bad weather wipes out the idea of the sun. The memory of light. Three days of grey skies and I can't picture anything else. Creeping through blurred-out scenes of a blind cave salamander.

When you don't have a job you don't have free time. Impossible to be a good producer or consumer, an economic subject. The dream of freedom clouds our work; later the ticks of the clock dig into our leisure.

The fate of a machine is to become a rusted piece of shit. The duality of equipment, the backside of our practicality obsessed selves. One flipped switch from losing all worth.

GOOD TIDINGS

THE DAYS SCATTER AND ROLL like billiard balls knocked from the table. One as irrecoverable as the other.

I shouldn't even call them days. It suggests an unreal unity. A day lurches from moment to moment and never meets itself. Gone before it arrives, sliding past its seconds. They call them seconds because there's no firsts; time is imaginary addition, a recounting. The original experience missing.

❦

The reason I work more than I should is that otherwise I wouldn't work enough. Time off has to pass like a night of bad sleep or it won't start up again.

I haven't worked a five-day week in a month. Now a full-time job looks like slavery. A month without serving and I expect strombolis to fly into my mouth. My laziness acts up. I need to be lashed with a bullwhip to carry on a ten-minute conversation.

New job won't start for at least another month. They're waiting on money from the investor. Owners of the business with two kids doing door dash and lyft to pay the bills until they can open the shop.

The gig economy, the bottom of the chum bucket service economy. African immigrants delivering Chinese plastic and Indian takeout to particle board apartment buildings put up by Hispanic migrants. A global game show. Compete for the chance to drop off marijuana laxatives on front porches. It's a little better than dying in a mud pit.

Less business for restaurants and shops on the holidays. Owners and managers wince over labor costs. They won't be happy until they've replaced you with a more recently arrived refugee, a screen, a dipping bird, a neon sign.

More administrators than ever and yet more downsizing and consolidating. Unemployment is low but no one wants to work. What should I do—I'm a free man paralyzed by limitless bad options. Go back to school, get another degree, go into the trades, get off the phone, make money on my phone, do what

I want, do what I don't want.

I need to convince people I don't like who don't like me to pay me to serve stupid overblown crap to other people I don't like who don't like me. The sputtering resentment economy. People's fuses are blown out. Everything you do is a bother; you're another hustler even when you're not. You feel yourself turn into a number with every email you send, every resume. Whatever it is: short story submissions, promotional posts, twitter messages, sex tape auditions. One more blockhead with a product.

My car's working again. It needed a new starter and battery. Only eight hundred bucks. It's for the best; I was going to blow that money on heat and electricity.

I went to visit my grandma in Plymouth, Indiana. She's ninety-two, with a cheerful spirit I can barely understand. Something curdled in my bloodline by the time I came out.

Half the family up north and half the family down south in a single state. People fly over Indiana but lengthwise it spans the northern hemisphere.

Late afternoon drive through dead croplands, in the diffuse light of a submarine sky. Bare woods and old farmhouses. A thousand tiny towns with names of other places. Birds flowing in and out of flocks.

My grandma had a gift card for Bob Evans so that's where we went. Bob Evans is owned by a capital group whose CEO is an Afghan guy. Down on the farm.

Right off Highway 31 in a strip mall with fast food and a

Wal-mart and a hair salon. The restaurant was nearly deserted and the manager looked like a medieval jailer. I ordered a burger. I should've eaten the laminated menu.

The contemporary small-town is a wasteland of simulacra. Commercial strips pumping out junk from nowhere, poisonous food and kitsch. A burial ground of local culture. A capitalist-soviet hybrid of machine diarrhea. Almost everyone from my grandma's generation is dead, has been dead for a long time, and most of her memory has already joined them.

But then it's the same with my connection to my own past, the place I grew up and the people I grew up with. I'm older than my own grandma, I've outlived myself. The current electro-urban environment deep fries the past and sends the message that there's nothing to look forward to either; nothing except amusing yourself right now with high-grade simulations that weakly remind you (or help you forget) that you were once capable of thinking and feeling in relation to actual people in your life.

Two hours north to see my grandma. Tomorrow I'm driving two hours south to see my parents. This way of life is a terminal illness; media is our morphine.

TUNNEL DAYS

The light from a sunless sky drapes the world in gray. Rain falls now and then. I'm walking on wet pavement with busted shoes. I have two hundred dollar hiking boots designed to stomp through a Siberian bog but each day I put on rotten sneakers pulled from a powerline. Rancid sock winter. Pond scum under my toenails. My feet smell like a flood at the dog pound.

Most of my days I'm alone. Something I share with plenty

of people I'd rather not meet. I've heard it called an epidemic of loneliness; a new manufactured disease from the expert class. Loneliness is suggested to us but finally we impose it on ourselves. We like how it feels, even when we cry about how much it hurts. Isolation has never been so accessible and seductive. Aristotle said a man who is content to live alone is either a beast or a god. That was before electronics. Before streaming shows and door dash and amazon delivery. Before dating apps, where the point isn't to find a mate, but to feel better about not having one. Today we slide into our solitude, good and lubed. The ancients would marvel at our toys of seclusion.

A beast or a god, or in our case, both. Living alone now makes us into mythological beings, hallucinated images of animal-gods.

More rain in the morning but the sky lets up in the afternoon. The atmosphere stays dark and metallic. I live inside a culvert. If this keeps up my eyes will shrink down to black beads and I'll sprout a tail.

I'm moving. That is to say, changing residence. Instead of packing my things and unpacking them in a new place, I'm going to burn my apartment to the ground. The landlord can keep the deposit. Staggering how a poor man heaps his trash. I need to get rid of most of what I own. The people who occasionally loot big box stores can sweep through my place. They won't take anything. My stuff is too old and dusty.

Renting: the worst of sedentary and nomadic living. From now on if I'm going to own something I'm going to be buried with it. A home should be a tomb or a tent. Freedom from people comes cheap, freedom from things is expensive.

HAUNTED BY HOSPITALITY

STUDIO APARTMENTS ARE JAIL CELLS where you're the inmate and the guard at the same time. I had to let myself out for the night. I'm getting no sleep. My cats sleep twenty hours a day except for the early morning stretch between twelve and four, when they train for an MMA tournament and the Kentucky Derby.

I booked a room at a Comfort Inn. Such places still exist. Hotels have drawn back behind the curtain; you don't see or hear much about them anymore. A whole sector of the economy invisible to the average eye. Especially the middling and lower end of hospitality, formerly respectable middle- and working-class accommodations. Chain hotels that cropped up in the early twentieth century to meet the travel needs of family vacationers and businesses, with standardized amenities and aesthetics that now emanate rootlessness and abandonment.

The hospitality industry supplies jobs. Plenty of people work in hotels, motels, and at tourist attractions. A marginal class with nothing to do but serve us when we want to move outside our normal circuits, feel like a different person, feel like no one.

All the labor and infrastructure we assume will be there for us any time we want a diversion. If not for the winding highways and buildings outfitted with plumbing and electrical systems, if not for the cleaners and front desk attendants working through all shifts, I wouldn't have been able to leave my apartment and spend the night in perfect isolation and anonymity.

When you stay in a hotel, you transform into an abstract version of yourself. A unit within a unit within units. Your features dissolve in the expertly designed blandness. What's left of your history unravels.

I've already forgotten what the sky was like when I drove to the Comfort inn. But I can see the man at the front desk; round with a red face and long white hair in a ponytail. The kind of guy who looks exactly like what he does, another example of the mysterious accord between organism and occupation in a world supposedly governed by chance.

Comfort Inns offer king-sized beds with oddly small pillows, a desk and two chairs. A bathroom with towels and a shower. A television in the center. The lighting was better than I expected. A little dialing and I had the room glowing.

Cable television has also receded from view and given ground to streaming entertainment and digital communication platforms. Channel surfing has been replaced by scrolling.

With cable, you can move laterally across channels, but you can't move vertically in time. You must watch the show when it runs, and if you want to record and replay it, you use a VCR, another archaic piece of equipment. The time slot of a show used to matter. Now, the release of a show or movie comes close to synchronizing an audience, but immediately after, the program is available for individualized consumption.

MTV still plays, along with other antiques of an outdated media complex. The music video represents a moment in the growing capture of artforms by the visual medium. A moment that has left us. It was said at the time that video killed the radio star; today streaming content has killed the video channel. You can still see these ghostly channels flickering in the hollows of commercial networks that have been surpassed by more advanced travel technology.

As everyone with a smartphone now stars in their own reality show, cable television's steady expansion of programs based on apparently real people prefigured the total inclusion of raw lives into the spectacle. Now the watcher of cable reality shows dates and derealizes himself, stepping back to a time of less comprehensive programming and surveillance.

Cooking shows and contests feature regular people pitted against each other for short-term glory and gain. Now the gameshow is digital technology and everyone is a contestant, with every statement and act competing for attention and money.

❧

I lie on the roomy bed and let the idiocy of the television soothe me. I imagined giving up and watching my way to the end. Television puts me into the atmosphere of a rest home; it's as if I no longer need to work, or even think. Everything has been done by someone else, and I'm only here to be amused, to forget ever having existed.

(The frail and sequestered elderly have little else but television. Entertainment not only fills in the free time of workers, it blunts the demoralization of those who no longer work.)

The night passed, I slept through it. I woke to a sunrise of faint purple coloring the sky just above a horizon of beige buildings and grey trees. A quiet parking lot except for the morning rush of trucks on the highway. I could've had breakfast at the Inn. The eggs and sausage looked like chew toys so I got a coffee and checked out.

Back to the apartment. The hell of not sleeping. I have a bottle of Zzzquil that says it's non-habit forming. Good to know. If I drank a bottle of Zzzquil every night for the rest of my life, it wouldn't mean I was addicted. I'll give it to my cats.

OUT ON A LIMN

THE EARTH CLEARS THE FROZEN CRUST from its eyes, kicks off its winter blanket. Late morning, new apartment. Light streams in like a pleasant memory. On the second story with hardwood floors and a fireplace. A peasant living in the country house of a king.

Grateful for the upgrade. Coming from a place with a broken toilet and a broken sink. Baseboard heaters that barely worked. Doorknobs that snapped off and missing fridge handles and shredded blinds and other slapstick defects; I went about the house like a silent comedy star, pulling drawers out of the dresser and slipping on unwashed socks, wrestling with the toilet to the tune of a ragtime piano.

Each day is the same as every other; each day is utterly alone with itself. Never touching another of its kind. The years lie behind us like desolate boardwalks, with cobwebbed concession stands and ferris wheels creaking in the wind. Whole lives spiral out, centers unto themselves but peripheral to everyone else. Boney toll booth attendants and flabby bus drivers with their own frayed outskirts, their thin social strands, the boring lore of their badly built worlds.

Everyone a hallway and a bridge and an alcoholic groundskeeper, a rusted conveyor belt and a smudged pair of spectacles with an outdated prescription, a half-empty toolbox, an unattended hardware store on a wasted town square. Marginally useful in ourselves but together we build an indomitable machine. Each of us brushes up against all other things and all other people without knowing anything about it.

In one moment, all is passage. The next instant, nothing moves, nothing succeeds.

I worked all weekend at the coffee shop. The old one, the most recent old one I left on good terms, as they say. I didn't commit the dreaded no-call no-show or punch a customer or take a dump on the counter so I'm still welcome to pick up shifts. I've needed them, what with moving expenses and trying to replace stolen shoes. I'm still waiting for my next job to start, and in the interim I've applied at numerous other jobs and contemplated other lives.

Jobs with descriptions emptied of concrete detail, mystical hype chants preparing me for interdimensional labor. Ayahuasca ad copy. Sketchy listings like email scams from the dial-up days. Nigerian princes needing someone in the American Midwest to run errands for them.

I almost took a substitute teaching job. Talked to a man on the phone. He prepared me for the onboarding process. I had to pay for a background check and a substitute license. Fill out several other forms. That was the end of that.

If they need a substitute teacher they can pay for my certificates and update my files and make sure I'm not a sexual predator on their own time and money. They're the ones with all the suspicions and qualifications, the burden should be on them. Modern work is often easier than almost everything people used to do, except in one crucial respect: getting the job. In the old days you could show up at a sawmill in ragged overalls and they'd hand you a shovel. You couldn't even write your name but you'd be working your ass off in seconds. Now you need a completed Saturday edition of the new yorker crossword and a personal reference from the pope to sit in a chair for eight hours and slowly stain your underwear.

I could work fourth shift at a FedEx warehouse, dropkicking packages of family heirlooms for twenty dollars an hour. But I'd have to take a piss test and finish a questionnaire. Attend training and orientation, fill out tax forms. Provide information on my bank account. I'd rather work right this second as a plague burier than write my social security number to get a job jacking off where I make millions.

EPILOGUE

ANOTHER JOB FELL THROUGH, collapsed like a house of toothpicks. I was going to manage a new shop, the latest new shop in a city stuffed with service. So many lattes and pastries, even Henry VIII would retire from the banquet.

One of those ambitious cafes with a market and a restaurant, breakfast and brunch and dinner. Funded by commercial real estate and tech investors also putting money into combat exoskeletons and shuttles to escape the earth. The strained artistry of the product motivated by a hysterical desire for approval, the false fuzzy business ethos disguising a simpering desire for control. They welcome all kinds except certain kinds. They like you if you tell them their miracle fruit frosting had you seeing God. If you disagree with their ideology they'd prefer you in a Latvian prison.

I must've been high on keyboard cleaner when I agreed to take the job. Responsible for a coffee menu, beer, wine, cocktails; training staff, teaching a new crop of employees, most of them fifteen years younger than me, a different breed, the last breed, raised on condescending video clips, with their unearned despair, their hand-me-down disasters, their aversion to work, their end of history presentation of self. The final flower of three generations of disowned seeds.

The owners wanted vulnerability, transparency, communication; for their sake, not mine. Applying interrogation and torture techniques with the lightest touch. They have ways of making you talk; they don't need thumbscrews or racks. Just repetition of terms, weepy tones. Insecure power needs you to placate its anxiety, help it sleep at night.

I can't manage an email account or an online profile, much less a whole staff, multiple menus. Nor did I feel like talking to them about my feelings. They fired me on their opening weekend.

But it's okay, because as soon as I fail, someone else fails and creates an opportunity. A man I worked for years ago, who let me stay a few nights in his nice house when my furnace broke in the freezing winter, his business went under. He sold his shops and works for a place he used to own, and they needed help.

Now I work next to a man who fired me and I feel nothing but soured pity, for him, for myself, for all the miserable creatures under the sun. All that labor in vain. All that digging and drilling to wind up on the same surface of nowhere. But it only feels like senseless toil if I stick to the modern idea of work as emancipation, work as a vehicle of self-discovery, history as progress, life as rich in possibilities and pregnant with triumphs. Rather, we work not to build wealth, to please ourselves and others, to increase comfort and diminish suffering, but to expiate our guilt, pay back the debt on our existence. For that purpose, any job is as good as any other, and I'm right where I need to be.

Caleb Caudell lives in Indianapolis. He is the author of a novel, *The Neighbor* (2021), and a collection of stories, *Novelty* (2023).

middleamericanliterature.substack.com

9 780645 776874